# *Forgotten Memories* SHATTERED DREAMS

ROBERTA WOOD ALLEN

WESTBOW
PRESS®
A DIVISION OF THOMAS NELSON
& ZONDERVAN

WestBow Press books may be ordered through booksellers or by contacting:

WestBow Press
A Division of Thomas Nelson & Zondervan
1663 Liberty Drive
Bloomington, IN 47403
www.westbowpress.com
844-714-3454

ISBN: 978-1-6642-7449-5 (sc)
ISBN: 978-1-6642-7451-8 (hc)
ISBN: 978-1-6642-7450-1 (e)

Library of Congress Control Number: 2022914191

Print information available on the last page.

WestBow Press rev. date: 08/17/2022

# *Forgotten Memories* SHATTERED DREAMS

ROBERTA WOOD ALLEN

WESTBOW
PRESS®
A DIVISION OF THOMAS NELSON
& ZONDERVAN

WestBow Press books may be ordered through booksellers or by contacting:

WestBow Press
A Division of Thomas Nelson & Zondervan
1663 Liberty Drive
Bloomington, IN 47403
www.westbowpress.com
844-714-3454

Scripture taken from the New King James Version® Copyright © 1982 by Thomas Nelson. Used by permission. All rights reserved.

ISBN: 978-1-6642-7449-5 (sc)
ISBN: 978-1-6642-7451-8 (hc)
ISBN: 978-1-6642-7450-1 (e)

Library of Congress Control Number: 2022914191

Print information available on the last page.

WestBow Press rev. date: 08/17/2022

# PROLOGUE

It has been almost two years since the accident that had claimed Jenny's precious memories. At first, she only learned about her past from those around her. After a while, bits and pieces of past experiences would come to her mind, yet they were all so hazy. Why could she not remember? It had been her life! She was the one who had lived it. Why did she have to piece it back together from other people's memories and perspectives? It was just so unfair. Some days she longed to forget everything just because it was so frustrating trying to remember. Some days she wore herself out trying to remember more, only to find that the things she thought she had set firmly in her mind would get cloudy again with the effort.

Today was one of those days. Something had triggered the briefest memory of a man who had obviously been very dear to her. What was it? A smell? A sound? A sight? She longed to figure out and capture whatever it was that had caused the vague remembrance. She longed to go back and drown herself in that smell, that sound, that thing that had brought an ever-so-fleeting picture of Ben back to her. Jenny's head ached with the effort. It was easier when she did not remember anything about him. It was easier when he was just a picture of a man painted by the opinions of others. It was easier when she did not have to deal with any of the feelings inside herself.

Lately, more and more images of Ben had been flashing through her mind. They came and went quickly, like unwanted scenes fast-forwarded in a movie and then just as quickly edited out. Jenny had trouble grasping them long enough to make sense of them. Although the images seemed to fade rapidly, the feelings they left behind lingered. It was the feelings, she soon discovered, that did not seem to fit into the puzzle.

Jenny's family had rallied around her after the accident. She moved back to her childhood home, back to the room she had slept in as a child.

The church family also rallied around her after the accident. She went back to the church she had attended as a child with her family, back to the place where she had developed such a deep faith in God.

In her head, Jenny knew that God rallied around her after the accident too, although she did not always feel it in her heart. She moved back into a close relationship with Him, a relationship that sustained her even now, when she still had so many unanswered questions.

Jenny's family had been patient to relive her past with her over and over again. In time, she actually began to remember some of the things they told her. Her church family was always quick to tell her how they marveled at her immovable faith in God, even as a teenager in the church. When other teens were making time for the world to creep into their lives, Jenny was steadfast in her commitment to her Lord. She weighed everything she did against how it would please or displease her Christ. In fact, some members told her that they had always expected her to become a missionary, "before the accident, of course."

Jenny was very thankful for her family at home and her family at church. She knew their prayers had played a huge part in her recovery. She was thankful for the blanks they filled in for her. Still, memories of Ben plagued her. Why would no one answer questions about him? Her own family and even those saints at church told Jenny that it was by God's grace that she did not remember some things about her life before that fateful night. While anxious to fill in the blanks about other aspects of her life, they seemed equally as anxious to keep details about this man from her.

But the time had come. There were too may unexplained feelings associated with Ben to be satisfied with the sparse details her family was willing to give her. It did not add up. Surely there was more to the story, and she had to know the truth. It was the only way to make sense of the battle going on inside her. So with her mind made up and determination as her fuel, Jenny vowed that tomorrow would be the day. She would start with her mom. Decision made, she let out a long sigh and drifted off to sleep.

# JENNY'S
*Story*

## CHAPTER

# 1

"Can you hear me? Wake up. Squeeze my hand if you can hear me." The words sounded like they were coming from a tunnel somewhere. *Is someone talking to me? Am I dreaming?* The pain in her head hurt so much she did not want to open her eyes. Then she heard the voice again, not so muffled this time, "Come on, squeeze my hand. That's a girl. Wake up and look at me."

Jenny struggled to open her eyes. She opened her eyes and looked up into the face of a man. He smiled ever so slightly and asked, "How do you feel?"

*How do I feel?* Jenny tried to focus. She opened her eyes once more, and the man asked again, "Can you tell me how you feel? Where does it hurt?"

"Oohhh … everywhere," Jenny whispered. "My head hurts really bad."

"It will be OK. Just relax. We have you immobilized on a backboard just to be safe, and we are taking you to the hospital. Try to stay awake. You have been in an accident, but we will be at the hospital soon. They will take good care of you."

With that, Jenny felt herself being lifted up and heard the stretcher slide easily into the ambulance. The lights were bright, and Jenny instinctively closed her eyes. Someone took her hand, and she heard the now familiar voice say, "My name is Ken, and we will be at the hospital very soon."

"What happened?" Jenny managed to whisper.

"It looks like the car slid off the road and into a ditch. You probably hit a patch of ice. What do you remember?" asked Ken softly.

Suddenly, panic began to set in. Jenny struggled to remember. All she could remember was hearing Ken's voice coming from a tunnel. *Why can't I remember?* Jenny wondered frantically. Tears welled up in eyes that already felt like they were on fire. Jenny began to moan and move about on the gurney.

"Shhhh." Ken tried to calm her down, but the more he tried to soothe her, the more Jenny panicked.

"I can't remember anything." She sobbed. "I can't remember anything."

"It's OK. It looks like you hit your head pretty good. It is not uncommon to lose your memory for a while. Rest, and try to relax. Let the doctors have a look at you. We are almost there."

Something about Ken's voice calmed Jenny, and she lay quietly. Although her eyes were shut, tears still streamed down her cheeks. Ken's hand wiped them away, and Jenny thought about how soft his hands were and how tenderly he touched her cheeks. He was good at the job he did. She was glad he was there.

The ambulance turned a corner, and the siren stopped. Funny that she had not even noticed the sound until it had stopped. Ken said, "Here we are. The doctors are waiting for you, and you will be in very good hands."

"Thank you," Jenny managed to whisper. The ambulance stopped. The doors opened, and Jenny could feel the stretcher being lifted out.

"Jenny … Jenny, honey. Are you OK?"

Jenny opened her eyes and sat up with a start.

"Mom?"

"Yes, dear. I thought I heard you crying. Is everything all right?"

Jenny looked around her cozy bedroom. "I guess I was just dreaming. I'm OK now."

Grace looked at Jenny and noticed that her bedclothes looked like she had been thrashing about. Jenny had not had a bad dream in a long time. They used to come often after she had been in that awful car accident, and Grace had hoped they were gone for good. She knew that any remembrance of the accident would bring more questions for her—questions she did not want to answer. She sighed ever so slightly, hoping afterward that Jenny had not noticed. "Well, I made coffee and was just about to make breakfast. What would you like for breakfast, Jenny?"

"Thanks, Mom, but I think I will grab a shower first. I'll just fix something a little later."

Grace turned to leave, and Jenny could hear her going back down the stairs. *Poor Mom,* she thought. Jenny had indeed heard the almost imperceptible sigh and noticed the look on her mother's face. It would not be a good day to ask questions. *No,* Jenny concluded, *I will have to wait until I can catch Mom off guard … catch her when she has not prepared herself to answer questions.* With that thought settled, Jenny headed for the shower.

CHAPTER

2

Dear Diary,
I had a dream about the accident last night. I hadn't had one in a long time. Maybe my determination to confront Mom about Ben triggered it. She must have heard me because she came in to check on me. So much for asking questions today. I still cannot figure out why no one will tell me about him. What is so awful that no one will talk about him? I guess I will never understand until I can remember for myself.

"Dear Lord, help me to remember."

Jenny got up from her desk. The shower had done wonders for her. She felt refreshed and ready to face the day ... even ready to face her mom. A new determination had built up inside her. Today may not be the day to ask questions of Mom, but there had to be *someone* who could give her enough information to trigger a memory. She just had to figure out where to start.

Jenny entered the kitchen. "Mmmm, that coffee sure smells good," she murmured as she poured herself a cup of the steaming black liquid. The cup was warm, and she cradled the warmth with both hands as she made her way to the breakfast nook.

Grace laid aside the new magazine she had been reading. "There's a great recipe for potato soup in here," she said as she gave Jenny one of those glances that begged for simple conversation.

Jenny smiled, slid onto the built-in bench that surrounded two sides of the well-worn little wooden table. "Are you thinking about soups already? It's barely fall."

Homemade soup was standard weekend fare at the Peterson home as soon as there was a hint of a chill in the air. As far back as Jenny could remember, there was always a warm Saturday pot of soup on the back burner of the stove, just waiting for someone to come in from the cold and take advantage of its bone-warming effects. Weekends were always family time, and there was never a strict schedule concerning meals and the like. With Mom and Dad both working while Jenny and her brother were growing up, meals during the week were planned, and everyone did their parts in putting them together. Jenny still, to this day, marveled at how her mom always managed to have a full-course meal on the table every weekday evening all those years. The weekends, however, were a different story. Saturdays were lazy days once the chores were done, and Saturday evenings in the fall and winter were most often spent in front of a warm fireplace with a nice, hot cup of homemade soup.

Grace turned back to her magazine. Jenny gently blew on her coffee and gazed out the window. It was funny how those memories of family weekends had come back to her so soon after the accident. It had been so scary in the hospital. She remembered being taken into the emergency room and having so many people surrounding her. They all looked alike in those green hospital scrubs. One person was taking vital signs and yelling them out as someone else started an IV. A doctor had shone a light in her eyes and told her to follow it with her eyes.

The next thing Jenny remembered about her hospital experience was waking up in a room. She was lost in thought as the memories played out in her mind.

An older nurse with a starched white cap was holding her wrist and taking her pulse. "Welcome back," she said as Jenny opened her eyes. "You have been sleeping for quite some time now. Your family is waiting outside to see you." The nurse checked the drip on Jenny's IV and wrote a few notes on a clipboard at the end of the bed. "I'll let the doctor know you are awake, and we will send your family in soon," she said as she disappeared through the door, closing it softly behind her.

Jenny looked around the room. It was a plain room. The walls were a light green color, and there was a TV near the ceiling at the end of her bed. On one side of her bed was a large window, although all she could see from her prone position was the sky. However, she could tell from the clear blue sky that it was a sunny day. On the other side of her was an empty bed. It was made up, and Jenny noticed how tightly the covers were tucked in all the way around. The spread covering the bed was a nondescript beige color, and there was a tray table straddling the bed.

It seemed only a few minutes had passed when the doctor arrived. He introduced himself as Dr. O'Brien as he fished his penlight out of his lab coat pocket. "How do you feel, Jenny?" he asked as he shined the little light into her eyes.

*Jenny. Is that my name?* It did seem kind of familiar, but in a funny sort of way. "How long have I been asleep?" she asked the doctor.

"About two days now," Dr. O'Brien replied. "Squeeze my hand." He took her hand in his.

She squeezed his hand and asked, "What happened? Why am I here, and why have I been asleep so long?"

"So many questions for someone who has just awakened," he replied in a bit of a brogue. "You had a little accident and bumped your head pretty badly. Your body has a way of mending itself as you sleep, and we kept a close eye on you. Other than a few scrapes and bruises, you seem to be on your way to a complete recovery. Do you remember being in an accident?" the doctor asked as he proceeded to poke her all over the place.

Jenny thought. "I seem to remember waking up and my head hurting a lot. Someone told me they were taking me to the hospital. I remember people being all around me. And then I woke up in here."

"Do you remember anything about the accident itself ... before you woke up with the headache?" The doctor felt Jenny's pulse begin to race.

"No," she said. "Why don't I remember it?"

He could see the tears well up in her eyes, but he had to know just how much she remembered of her life before the accident. "Jenny," he said, "tell me where you live."

"I don't know," Jenny said and sobbed. "I can't remember!"

By now Jenny was really panicking, and the doctor tried to soothe her. "Shhhh... it's OK. You took a nasty hit on your head, and it's not

uncommon to experience short-term memory loss. Relax. It will probably all come back to you soon. The best thing to do is to rest, and let the healing process take place. As you mend, things will begin to come back to you. Would you like to see your family?"

"Jenny, your coffee has gotten cold," Grace said gently. "Where is your mind, girl? You looked like you were a million miles away."

"Oh, I was just thinking about the fall and about how much I always look forward to your homemade soups," Jenny lied. "The leaves are already turning colors and will soon fill the yard. I think fall is my favorite time of the year."

"I like fall too. Would you like me to warm that coffee for you?" Grace asked as she reached for Jenny's cup. "I think I need a refill myself. What are your plans for the day?" she asked as she swept across the room.

*My plans?* Jenny thought. *Well, my plans are to get out of this house and talk to some people. I need some answers, and today is the day I begin to look for them.* "Oh, I think I will drive into town and see if I can find a good book at the library. Maybe I will stop by Killary's and see if that red sweater is still on sale. All this talk of fall is making me want a new fall outfit. How about you?"

"I am meeting Mary at the church this morning. We are going to sort through those clothes that were donated and see if we can find some sweaters and jackets to take down to the homeless shelter. I should be home around 1 o'clock, and I think I just might try out that new potato soup recipe," she said as she set Jenny's coffee cup down in front of her. "Yes, I think today is a good day for soup."

CHAPTER

3

There did seem to be a nip in the air as Jenny scurried out to her car. It was one of those refreshingly crisp days that were so welcome following the dog days of summer. Jenny's car was one of those new Volkswagen Bugs, although it wasn't quite new. She had bought it secondhand from one of her dad's friends, whose son had grown tired of it and gotten something just a little more classy. She had seen so many pictures of and heard so many stories about the old-style VW Bug that her mom and dad had when they were first married that it seemed only natural to choose one for her own.

She started the car and bowed her head for a moment:

> Dear Lord,
> I praise You for this day and for the crispness in the air. You are a mighty and awesome God. I know You want the best for Your children, and that means You want the best for me. You were faithful in healing my body and for bringing back so much of my memory, and I thank You for that.
>
> You know how much I have been struggling lately with the things I still cannot remember. The more people do not tell me, the more I want to know. Please direct my paths, O Lord. Help me to hear Your voice and see Your ways. If I am meant to remember, please show me where to

start. But if I am meant to forget, please take this longing to know from my heart.

You know best, Lord, and I trust You in this. Amen.

Jenny slowly backed out of the driveway and headed for town. And "town" it was. No big-city living for the Petersons. With the exception of the four years she had spent away at college, Jenny had lived all of her life in this small town. Even the college town she lived in would be considered small by most people's standards, but it had seemed like the big city to this small-town girl.

There were two stop signs and a yield sign between Jenny's street and Main Street. Main Street actually had a couple of traffic lights. At the second light, Jenny turned down Maple Street. She had heard a saying once about how cities tore down trees to build streets and then named the streets after trees. But that was not the case with Maple Street. Huge maples lined both sides of the street. In the summer, it was almost dark traveling down that street under the canopy of fully dressed maple branches. In the fall, the leaves covered the short street and kept the street sweeper very busy. Jenny noticed that the first of God's glorious "litter" had begun to fall to the street.

Without even thinking about where she was going, Jenny turned into the parking lot of the library. It must have been her conscience that directed her there. After all, didn't she tell Mom that she was going to the library today? She chuckled to herself and pulled into a parking spot near the front door. How many hours had she spent inside the little wood-shingled library during her childhood years? The curator of the library was an old family friend, and he encouraged Jenny to take many literary adventures. She would never forget when she first discovered the *Borrowers* series. What fun to go on adventures under the floorboards with Arietty! With not much else around Harborview to entertain a young child, she spent many hours at the library, developing a love for books that she carried with her even now.

She opened the library door, and the musty smell of old building mingled with old books greeted her warmly. There was a tiny area just inside the front door, barely enough room to step around the open outer door and close it before opening an adjacent door, which led into the library itself. She smiled as the entryway floor creaked as if welcoming her to familiar territory. Stepping across the well-worn threshold, she saw Carleton look up from the book on his desk. She remembered how old he had looked to her as a child and thought, *He is probably as ancient as some of the books in this treasure trove.* Still, he was a welcome sight to this home-town girl.

"Hi, Carleton," Jenny said, giving him a smile.

"Well, Jenny," Carleton said with a twinkle in his eye. "Long time, no see. Did that fancy college library spoil you?"

"No, of course not, Carleton. You know no other library could ever replace this one. This one is like home to me."

"So why haven't you been around here since you came back home?" Leave it to Carleton to speak his mind.

Jenny thought she saw a frown cross his face when he asked the question. But at the same time, she realized just how long it had actually been since she visited her childhood refuge. "I guess I've had other things on my mind for the last year or so. But that is no excuse. I promise to come and visit you more regularly from now on. Am I forgiven?"

"I'll have to think about that one," Carleton replied, the twinkle once more in his gray-blue eyes. "What are you looking for here today, Jenny?"

"Oh, I don't really know. I think the change in the weather has put me in the mood to curl up in front of the fire with a good book. Any suggestions?"

"Well, you know where to find the newest additions to the library. Or at least you should know. But then you usually took all the new things home to read before they ever actually hit the shelves—if I am remembering correctly. That was you, wasn't it?"

Jenny giggled. Carleton made her feel like that little girl again, anxiously waiting for him to open the latest shipment of new books. "It might have been," she returned the easy banter with her old friend.

"So what have you been reading lately?" he asked with only a slightly more serious tone.

"Mom has kept me pretty well supplied with new books from the church library. Did you know she has been volunteering as the church librarian? She said she was getting too restless alone in that house after she retired, so she set out to find things to occupy her time. With her love for books, the library was the perfect outlet for her energy, and it filled up just enough of her time that she could enjoy her retirement and still feel like she had accomplished something useful during the week. I think she pretty much rearranged the whole thing. There was a budget for books and supplies so she has been buying a lot of new items and cataloging them herself. She kept bringing them home to work on and I merely took advantage of the situation." Jenny became unusually quiet after realizing she had been rambling on and on. After some awkward silence, Jenny laughed nervously and then said in a more serious tone, "I'm sorry that I did not at least come by to say hello."

"That's OK. I understand," Carleton said with a look of compassion on his face. He had heard of her accident, of course, as if in a town this size there was anyone who had *not* heard about it. It was big news to a small town. When nothing much happens around town, anything that does happen immediately becomes newsworthy and tends to stay newsworthy until something else replaces it. He had also heard that she had lost her memory and assumed she had merely forgotten about all the time she had spent in the library as a child.

Sensing there was more that Carleton was not asking about, Jenny decided to take the lead. Perhaps a conversation with Carleton would open that door Jenny was hoping to find. Maybe this was the place Jenny was looking for to begin her quest for the missing pieces to her memory.

"So what have *you* been up to since I saw you last?" she began. "How long has it been anyway?"

"Well, let me think." He tilted his head to one side. "You came in here during the summer break right before you went back to school for your last semester. Seems like I remember you saying something about wishing you had majored in library science instead of early education." His smile, which made those eyes look like they had little silver stars in them, slowly played across his face.

"Carleton, if that was a test of my memory, you win. I really did think about going back to college, majoring in library science, and making it a double degree. I even went to the counselor to ask what it would take to complete the double major. You know, I had forgotten about that until you mentioned it just now."

"I heard that you had lost your memory after the accident, Jenny.

Figured that was what was keeping you away from here," Carleton replied hesitantly. He never was one to pull any punches. One could usually count on him to say just what he was thinking.

"I did stay in the house for a long time after it happened. It was strange not being able to remember some things, but most of it has come back now," Jenny replied. "I think I'll check out those new books."

Why did she stop the conversation there? What was she doing walking away? It seemed like she was getting somewhere. At least Carleton seemed to be talking to her without holding back. *Jenny,* she admonished herself, *you are going to have to persevere much better than that if you ever expect to accomplish anything!* But she could not bring herself to turn around and try to pick up the conversation where they left off.

Walking over to the bookshelves toward the front of the main lobby area, Jenny scooped up a couple of the new books. They had been standing partially open and strategically placed on top of the shelves, right where they could catch the eye of patrons entering the library. She took the books and settled down in a far corner by the front window in one of the two overstuffed armchairs that had been there as long as she could remember. She fingered the books but did not really pay much attention to them. Carleton had said just enough to put her into one of her remembering moments.

It had been awful waking up in the hospital and not knowing who she was. Jenny remembered the doctor saying her name, and it sounded so strange and yet familiar at the same time. He had asked if she wanted to see her family and when they came into the room everyone was a stranger to her. They must have been able to tell from her response that she did not know who they were. She supposed now that the doctor had warned them before they had come into the room. Her mom and dad both had tears in their eyes, and Jenny had inadvertently stiffened when they tried to hug her.

Over the next few days, family and friends she did not recognize filled her waking hours. Looks of hurt and concern on their faces troubled Jenny as she struggled to remember who she was, who they were. With trepidation, they answered her questions and valiantly tried to comfort her.

The doctor promised her memory would return as Jenny healed but until then, conversations remained awkward and strained. She could tell that they all wanted to help her remember, but they remained strangers to her. It is hard to trust a stranger. It is even harder to trust that those strangers are your family and friends.

In time, the doctor's prognosis had proven correct. Before she even left the hospital, Jenny began to recognize and remember family members and close friends. She remembered some places. She remembered some events. She still did not remember the accident itself, and the time frame preceding the accident was still a blur. But after finally being released from the hospital and on her way home, she breathed a sigh of relief when the streets looked familiar. The buildings and even the trees all seemed to beckon to her with a welcome familiarity as she watched them pass by the car window. When Dad pulled the car into their driveway, Jenny let out her breath, only then realizing that she had been holding it all the way down her street. The house, her home, was just as she remembered it. Uncontrollable happy tears slid down her cheeks as Dad parked the car and opened her door.

"Jenny, are you all right?" Carleton asked as he stooped down and looked in her face.

Tears were streaming down Jenny's cheeks as she smiled up at him. "Yes, I'm fine. I was just reliving some happy memories. God is so faithful," she said. "He is just so good to us."

"Hmmm," Carleton muttered under his breath as he headed back. He did not put nearly as much stock in God as Jenny and her family did. His philosophy had always been that people were responsible for their own well-being. *Well, to each his own,* he thought as he settled back behind his desk.

Jenny watched him as he scuffed across the well-worn oak floor. The wide dark-wood planks that made up the floor seemed to cushion his steps all the way. *A fitting floor for a library,* she thought. Not even a creak in a room created for silent reading and reflection. Glancing at her watch, Jenny realized she had been sitting in the old armchair for nearly an hour. So much for her quest. With new resolve, she rose to cross the room. On her way back to the front desk, Jenny replaced the books she had picked up. She looked over at Carleton and saw that he had picked up the local newspaper. Why hadn't she thought about that before? *Maybe there was some useful information in the newspaper archives about the accident. Surely the story had made the local newspaper.*

The library had once been a house, about 110 years ago. It was a landmark in the town and owned by the family of one of the original settlers. When the last owner passed away, it was discovered that he left the homestead to the local historical society in the hope that it would be preserved for future generations. Carleton's grandfather had begun the library in the main room of the house many years ago. And as the library grew, the other rooms began to be used to shelve the books. Now all the rooms on the first floor were library rooms. A large attic room upstairs eventually became the storage and office area as the main floor gave way to its treasure trove of literature. A sleeping area, a mini-kitchen, and a bathroom had been added up there in subsequent years. Carleton had moved into the attic efficiency when his wife died nearly ten years ago. It would be fitting for Carleton to spend his remaining years surrounded by this bit of history.

Jenny went to the back of the library, into what was probably at one time the kitchen area of the home. A back door led out to a patio of sorts made up of slate pieces fitted into the ground and worn smooth over the years. The back door was kept locked these days; the only entrance to the library remained the front door. There was a large wooden trestle table in the middle of the floor and racks all around the outside walls with newspapers and magazines hanging on them like quilts on quilt racks. They hung there about a month, and then the newspapers were transferred to microfiche. Jenny sat down at the microfiche archives and began to search the local papers from two years ago.

It didn't take her long to find the story concerning her accident. The headline simply read, "Local Girl Hurt in Automobile Accident." Jenny read on:

> Jennifer Peterson, daughter of Dr. and Mrs. Gregory Peterson of Harborview, was hurt in a single-car accident on Old Route 3 on Friday night, January 3. Ms. Peterson

had been traveling to her parents' home after visiting her brother in upstate New York. She was the only person in the vehicle. Police officers on the scene reported that the car apparently skidded off the main road and into a ditch. They blame the accident on the icy road conditions.

Ms. Peterson was transported to a local hospital with a head injury and is listed in serious but stable condition. Her mother, Grace Peterson, confirms that Jenny had slipped into a coma but is expected to come out of it at any time. Doctors are optimistic about a full recovery. Family and friends are keeping vigil at her bedside at Blufftown Hospital.

Members of Harborview Community Church are having a prayer service for Jenny on Sunday at 10:00 a.m., before their regular 11:00 a.m. worship service. The church extends an invitation to any members of the community who wish to join them.

*Well,* thought Jenny, *now I know as much as I already knew.* So much for small-town newspaper reporting. Of course, if it had happened in a larger city, it probably would not have made the news at all! But here in Harborview, it had been big news.

Jenny reread the short article and smiled at how impressive the reporter had made it sound. "Dr. and Mrs. Gregory Peterson." Her father probably had not taken too kindly to that. He was so down-to-earth that titles did not impress him much. He always said that people would think he was a medical doctor and tell him about every ache and pain if he went by Dr. Peterson. Although a humble man, Gregory Peterson did take some pride in the PhD he had earned. He worked long and hard to accomplish the degree while working full time and supporting a family. Jenny could still remember the celebration at home when he was awarded the degree and the title that went with it. She was about ten years old, as she recalled. Her brother, Richard, must have been about fourteen then. They had helped Mom make a special dinner and had decorated the dining room with handmade posters and streamers. It had been a traditional Peterson family celebration. The memory was as clear in Jenny's mind as if it had happened yesterday. All the more frustrating for her on this new quest to fill in so many other blank spots.

Jenny turned off the microfiche reader and headed back to the main library room. *This had been a waste of time. I must be bolder,* she thought as she crossed the threshold and caught sight of Carleton. Jenny had been brought up to be quiet and reserved and to mind her own business. Asking probing questions was definitely not in her comfort zone. It would be akin to gossiping or backbiting or butting into someone else's affairs. *But,* she reasoned, *these are my affairs, and if I am ever going to find answers, I have to ask questions!* She took a couple more steps and paused again. Carleton was always one to speak his mind. He would answer her questions—if she could just bring herself to ask them.

"Jenny, I wondered where you had gone. I thought you might have left without saying goodbye."

Here was her chance. It was now or never.

"No, I was in the back room, looking at some old newspaper articles," she said avoiding eye contact. "I was actually trying to find out some details about my accident." She looked up just a little and tried to gauge Carleton's reaction.

Carleton just took it all in stride. It seemed Jenny was the only one having trouble here.

"What exactly were you looking for?" he asked.

"Oh, I don't know for sure. Whatever it is that no one is telling me, I guess. It's just, well, I had a dream last night. Every time I dream about the accident, I have new questions about stuff I still don't remember."

"I thought you said your memory had returned," Carleton said with a lift of his eyebrows. "What kind of stuff do you think you are still not remembering?"

*This is getting me nowhere,* Jenny thought. *I'm just going to ask him outright.*

"Carleton, do you remember a man named Ben?"

"Of course I do."

Jenny's hopes began to soar.

"There's Ben Carpenter down at the transmission place and Ben Mott over at the VFW. Which Ben are you talking about?"

"No, I mean," Jenny searched for words. "Do you know someone named Ben who might have been a friend of mine? I keep remembering the name but cannot put a face with it. I don't remember anything else. Just a name. But, sometimes, things … or something will remind me of this person. Or a feeling I had toward him … and … and," Jenny stammered. "Well, it's just so frustrating not being able to remember!" Tears welled up in her eyes, and she turned away. "I guess I need to be running along now."

"Now hold on a minute there. Not so fast." Carleton came around the desk to stand beside her. "Let's have a talk about this Ben who you can't remember but at the same time makes you cry. Let's go over there and sit down," he said, nodding toward the overstuffed armchairs. "My old legs won't let me stand for very long at one time these days."

Jenny took a Kleenex from the box on the desk and reluctantly followed the aged man to the familiar corner. He sat in the far chair, and Jenny settled herself in the one closer to the window. She began to pick at the Kleenex in her hand. Slowly she looked up into Carleton's eyes. How many times over the years had they sat in this library and talked of faraway places that only books could make come alive? How many times had he sat and listened to her talk of going away to college? How many times had he taken the time to help her find just the right book to match her mood? Why was it so hard to talk to him now? Why was it so hard to talk to anyone about this elusive Ben? It made no sense.

Carleton sat quietly, expectantly. Determination fueled Jenny's resolve and she began. "I don't know how to explain it. When I woke up in the hospital, I didn't even know my own name. Everyone around me was a stranger. I didn't even know my own family. The doctors kept telling me my memory would return. By the time I left the hospital, I was able to remember my family and my friends. Things and places were familiar to me. I was so relieved when Dad brought me home and I actually recognized the house!"

The Kleenex in Jenny's hand was beginning to look a bit frayed. But with a comforting nod from Carleton, she continued. "Mom and Dad and Richard would fill me in on all kinds of stuff, and soon I felt like I was remembering on my own. But I still did not remember the accident or the events surrounding it. I know I was coming from Richard's house, but I still don't remember the time I spent there. They tried to tell me stuff, but it was like a story and not like a memory."

She paused. Carleton nodded and smiled at her. "Anyway," Jenny had nearly shredded the Kleenex by now, "I keep remembering a man named Ben, but no one will tell me anything about him. Mom and Dad tell me it is better that I do not remember him. The few people at church whom I ask say they do not know any Ben. Then they tell me what a blessing it is that I do not remember some things—that God will allow me to remember what He wants me to remember and that I have to trust Him. They tell me that God sometimes blots stuff out of our memories that would be too painful for us to remember, and that is why I don't remember the accident itself." She paused only slightly before softly adding, "But when I remember Ben's name, I don't feel like it is a painful memory."

Jenny was feeling much bolder now that she had finally began to let it all out. The Kleenex had become an unrecognizable pile of confetti. "So since my family will not tell me about Ben, and the people at church do not seem to know anything about him, I am trying to find out anything I can about the accident in hopes that by remembering something new, it will trigger the memories I still cannot recover. I am hoping to somehow conjure up an image of a face to go with the name. I just don't really know where to start. Mom gets so upset when I bring it up, and Dad only seems to shut me out. I don't see Richard much, but he wouldn't tell me anything when he was here to visit last."

Jenny realized that she was not really talking to Carleton anymore but was now just thinking out loud. Maybe that was the catalyst she needed to get her started ... to say all of this out loud.

She looked up at Carleton, and the familiar twinkle was in his eyes. His smile was just a little one-sided. He knew she had made a breakthrough. "Well, Jenny," he said with a grin, "I think you have just taken your first step to finding out all you want to find out. I don't know who this Ben of yours is, but it will be an interesting road you have set out on. You can do this. I have every confidence in you."

"Thanks, Carleton," Jenny said as she rose to leave. Carleton stood and gave her an unexpected, encouraging, father-like hug. "Go get 'em, tiger."

Jenny realized that she had indeed taken a first step in a no-turning-back adventure. She was not sure where the trip would take her, but she knew she was ready for the journey. She gave Carleton a hug in return. Then with a smile and a wave, she was on her way.

Jenny left the library with a new spring in her step. *There,* she thought, *it is out in the open. I said it all out loud to someone who did not discourage me.* The fact was that she had been entirely boosted by Carleton's encouragement. *Lord,* she thought, *leave it to You to use someone who does not have much faith in You to encourage the one who is supposed to be so full of faith. You really do have a sense of humor, don't You?*

She couldn't help smiling as she opened the door to the VW and got inside. Did the sky look just a little clearer? Was the sun shining just a little brighter? Had the leaves turned a bit more colorful? Was she going to stay in her seat or just float above the car on the way home? It was turning into a perfect day. Maybe she would go to Killary's after all. She felt like celebrating!

# CHAPTER

# 4

It was after six o'clock before Jenny pulled into the driveway at home. Mom and Dad would be wondering what had happened to her. Try as she might she could not convince them that she wasn't a little girl anymore. She was a grown woman who had already spent four years away from home while attending college. Maybe they had become a little more protective of her because she had moved back home to recuperate after the accident. She had not given it much thought before now, but maybe, just maybe, this new quest of hers should include leaving the nest and finding a place of her own.

"Hello, I'm home," Jenny shouted as she closed the front door. She could smell the fireplace and knew she would find her parents in the family room, enjoying the first fire of the season. Mom must have made the soup.

"Jenny, where have you been all this time? We were so worried." It was Grace, who got up and met her in the doorway of the family room as though Jenny had been gone for a week instead of a few hours. "You said you were going to the library and to Killary's. I called the library, and Carleton said you left a couple of hours ago. Are you all right?"

"I'm fine, Mom. In fact, I am more than fine!" Jenny just kind of danced her way past her mother and into the family room.

Gregory Peterson had stood up and was now watching her curiously. "I tried to tell her you would be OK," he said, glancing at his wife. One look from her mom told Jenny that Dad had been as worried as Mom, but since

Jenny was home safely, he did not have to show it. It was typical Dad, but it did not matter. It would take more than that to quench the good mood that had settled over this newly liberated Jenny.

"Mmmmm, the fire smells so good. I hope you made the soup, I'm starving," Jenny said as she smiled at both of them. She had noticed that both set soup mugs down on the coffee table on her arrival. "I am home safe and sound, but I just may faint from hunger if I don't get some of your soup in me soon," she teased.

"I'll get you a cup of soup, Jenny. Why don't you hang up your coat and get warm in front of the fire. I'll be right back," Grace said as she moved toward the kitchen.

"OK, Mom, thanks," Jenny said as she sloughed her coat off her shoulder. She had forgotten she still had her purse on her shoulder and the Killary's bag in her hand. She set them down on the sofa so she wouldn't have to juggle them while she took off her coat and headed to the closet. "By the way, I found a beautiful sweater at Killary's," she shouted over her shoulder in the general direction of the kitchen. "It's red!"

"Didn't you just buy a new red sweater?" Gregory asked as Jenny settled on the sofa.

"Well, Dad, a girl cannot have too many red sweaters, you know," she replied. She smiled. The last time she had bought a red sweater was her last Christmas in college. That was nearly two years ago now.

"Here's your soup, Jenny. Do you want the afghan to throw over your legs?" Grace asked, hovering over Jenny like the mother hen she was.

"No, Mom. I'm fine. This sure smells good. I am sure it will warm me up in no time," Jenny said as she wrapped her hands around the steaming mug. *Yes, this is nice*, Jenny thought, *but I think I may be ready for a place of my own.*

CHAPTER

5

Dear Diary,

Yesterday turned out to be a wonderful day. I did not realize just how frustrated I have been. When I opened up and talked to Carleton, it is like a weight was lifted off my shoulders. I don't know any more now than I did before, but I have a new outlook on the whole situation. I have decided that Mom and Dad are probably the only ones around here who know anything about Ben. They, for sure, are not going to be of any help. I have to try to piece together facts from someplace else. I thought about it all night and have decided to ask Dad if I can go back to Montague with him this week. Maybe I can find out something there.

Dear Lord,

The more time passes, the more I am convinced that I am not meant to forget. I trust You to answer my prayers, and I have prayed that if I am not to remember, that You remove this desire to know. Yet with each passing day, the desire grows stronger and stronger. I am convinced that You mean for me to remember. So, Lord, guide me in my search for answers. Lead me to people and places that will jog my memory. Somehow, lead me to Ben.

There was a soft knock on Jenny's bedroom door. Grace poked her head in around the door. "Jenny, honey, it is nearly nine o'clock. You had better hurry if you want to eat breakfast before we leave for church."

"I'm ready now. How do you like my new sweater?" Jenny asked as she started toward the door. "It was still on sale yesterday, and it goes so well with my black slacks. Think Dad will notice?" Jenny giggled as she told her mother about the comment Gregory had made the evening before. With a knowing smile, Grace linked arms with her daughter, and the two of them walked down the hallway toward the stairs.

Gregory Peterson was sitting in the breakfast nook with the newspaper in front of his face and a cup of black coffee growing cold on the table. He seemed engrossed in some article when the women came in. Grace nodded toward her husband of some thirty years and whispered to Jenny, "I doubt he will even notice that we have come into the room, let alone what we are wearing today."

Jenny couldn't resist the temptation. She sat down on the wooden bench kind of backwards and scooted herself over toward her dad. She leaned in across his lap, put her head under his arm that was holding one side of the newspaper, and poked her head up right in front of the newspaper. She used to do that a lot as a little girl, and for some reason, she could not resist the urge to do it again. The look on her father's face was priceless! He surely did not expect that move.

"Well, ah, good morning, Jenny," he sputtered, trying to gather his wits about him. Grace and Jenny burst into laughter, but Gregory quickly recovered from the shock and decided to play along. "What's Daddy's little girl up to today?" he cooed to Jenny, just like he used to when she was four years old. "Give your old dad a big kiss." He proceeded to plant a sloppy, wet kiss on her cheek as he tousled her hair playfully.

"Dad," Jenny protested, "my hair!" With that, everyone broke into another round of laughter. Jenny's auburn hair was a mass of tight curls, and she "combed" her hair by shaking her head. There was no way to actually get a brush through the mass of spirals, although she did make the attempt from time to time. Jenny looked good in her shoulder-length tresses. They framed her face in a flattering way, and the coloring only enhanced the sea-green eyes that, at the moment, were sending playful tears down her cheeks as she struggled to break free of her dad's massive hug.

"Come on, you two," Grace pleaded through stifled chuckles. "We are never going to make it to church on time this way."

CHAPTER

6

Harborview Community Church was a small church with a family atmosphere. The building itself had belonged to another family of original settlers. It had once been a house, but over a hundred years ago, the family made arrangements for the building to be used as a church, and as long as it continued to be used as a church, it remained a sort of community property. If the time came when it was no longer used as a church, ownership somehow reverted back to the descendants of the original owners. Jenny never did quite know exactly how the whole thing had been arranged. It had been a church for as long as she could remember. Her mom had grown up in the church there, and probably her mom before her. It did not seem comprehensible that it could ever not be a church.

There was no parking lot as such, so drivers just pulled their cars off the road up and down the street. There were not many curbs along country roads, and the roadside grass showed the telltale signs of cars having parked on it. Somehow the scene lent a bit of country charm to the area. Woods bordered the church on either side, so the worn grassy area along the street meshed in well with the less-than-perfectly manicured countryside. The congregation was small, as often happens in small country towns, so the parking arrangements had never needed to be addressed. Jenny couldn't help but think about the areas around campus at Montague with the curbs and finely trimmed lawns. She much preferred the country look.

There was a bit of a retaining wall immediately in front of the church, and two worn concrete steps led up from the roadside to the concrete walk that, in turn, led to the front door of the church. The bell that normally hung in the small steeple was currently at rest on the church lawn to the right of the walkway while some repairs were being made to the building. Even that could not take away from the charm of the little country church.

As one walked inside the front door, there was a small area on either side, about three feet deep, from the outside of the church to the inner wall, where the sanctuary began. One side of this area had bookshelves holding hymnals against the end wall and coat hooks along the front wall and the back wall. The other side had coat hooks on all three walls, but there was also a long rope hanging down from the ceiling. This was the rope used to ring the bell as a call to worship when it was properly residing in the steeple and not lying on the front lawn, of course. It was in front of the rope that Pastor Tom stood and greeted each person by name as they entered. Jenny briefly thought about some of the bigger churches she visited while away at college. They all had contemporary features and up-to-date designs, yet with all their bells and whistles, they could not hold a candle to a little country church where the members worshipped as a family. The white clapboard outside, contrasting with the old, dark, worn oak on the inside, added to the ambiance of the whole worship experience.

And then there was that smell. It was not a bad smell. Jenny unconsciously breathed deeply as she thought of the scent. Perhaps it was the old wood or maybe the polish used on the old wood. Perhaps it was the old kerosene heater. Perhaps it came from the candles or the fresh flowers that someone always made sure were on the altar each Sunday. Perhaps all the scents just came together in an indescribable fragrance that Jenny would always associate with this little country house of worship. And maybe, just maybe, it was also a pleasing aroma to the Lord they all worshipped there.

"Good morning, Petersons," greeted Pastor Tom in his bass voice. "Isn't it a beautiful day for worship? Grace and Jenny, you are looking lovely this morning as usual," the pastor continued in a tone of voice that evoked the picture of a gentleman sweeping off his cap and bowing in a grand manner. Pastor Tom gripped Gregory Peterson's hand in a firm handshake and told him how very blessed he was to be escorting two such lovely ladies.

"You're absolutely right, Pastor," Gregory agreed as he smiled and gripped the pastor's shoulder with his free hand. "Absolutely right!"

Jenny noticed a hint of rose coloring her mother's cheeks as she smiled sweetly at the pastor and thanked him. Even working out in the world all those years had not robbed Grace of her humility. "I hope I mature as gracefully as you," Jenny whispered to her mother as they slid into the third pew from the front.

Of course, this caused another rush of color to Grace's cheeks, but the sparkle in her eyes told Jenny that the compliment meant a great deal to her. The fact that her daughter wanted to be like her brought just enough pride to her humble heart to keep Grace human, like the rest of the mortal race, with her feet planted firmly on the ground.

Jenny slid over in the pew, closer to the wall and the window that looked out over the side lawn. In her periphery she could see the bell lying there and suddenly missed the familiar call to worship that sounded from that bell as a normal part of their Sunday mornings. About fifteen minutes before the service would begin, Pastor Tom would ring the bell and then take his position in front of the rope to greet the folks as they came in to worship. Jenny wondered why she had not missed the sound the last few Sundays since the bell had been taken down. Why was she waxing so nostalgic as she sat in church this morning? Could this all be part of her liberation? Could these thoughts be connected to the idea of moving out on her own that had been taking shape in her mind as she began this quest to rediscover those remaining lost memories?

Music sounded, and Jenny was summoned out of her reverie and back to the present. Miss Olford was playing the organ, and the music was sweet as it filled the tiny sanctuary. Jenny hummed along with the familiar tune. Pastor Tom, now in his seat at the front of the church, watched as Miss Olford coaxed the beautiful strains out of the old pipe organ. He had a smile on his face as he, too, drank in the melody as if it were music from heaven itself. Way too soon the last note reverberated in the tiny room, and a reverent silence followed. Pastor Tom hesitated as he approached the podium. After a thoughtful moment, he gazed at the congregation in an all-encompassing, sweeping gaze and said, "And now for the invitation."

There were a few smiles and a couple of "Amens" from the pews as the pastor, in those few words, had managed to summarize the atmosphere in that place. People had come to worship that morning, and the music had already summoned their willing hearts into the presence of a holy God. As if wanting to preserve the moment, Pastor Tom hesitated once more before praying his opening prayer:

> Lord, we humbly come into Your presence this morning. We thank You for joining us here today. Please cleanse our hearts, and make us worthy to worship You. Still our spirits, and make us revel in Your holiness. Quiet our minds that we may hear You speak. May You find our worship pleasing in Your sight. Above all else, Lord, glorify Yourself here today. In Your most holy name, we pray. Amen.

"Mmmm, would you pass those potatoes back this way?" Gregory asked. "They taste extra good today. What did you do differently, hon?"

Grace smiled and gave Jenny a look that told her they were the same old potatoes she always made. "I don't think I did anything differently, dear." And then, as if suddenly remembering there was a guest at the table, Grace blushed once again and added, "I guess you are just extra hungry today."

"Hmm, well, whatever you did, keep on doing it because these are the best potatoes ever," muttered Gregory as he heaped another generous portion onto his plate.

"Maybe it's because we are eating Sunday dinner at home today," Jenny offered.

As a general rule, they stopped at the diner on the way home from church on Sundays. It was an old habit from when Grace and Gregory both worked all week. Gregory always said Sunday was a day of rest, and his wife deserved to be out of the kitchen. So it became a weekly tradition to eat Sunday dinner at the local diner. Even after Grace retired, the tradition lingered. But the pastor was joining them for dinner today, so Grace had prepared a real home-cooked meal. She had reasoned that even though the diner had good food, the pastor was a single man and probably did not get a lot of home cooking. She must have been right in her reasoning because Pastor Tom seemed to be enjoying his meal immensely. Joining in the conversation, he said, "Grace, these potatoes are marvelous, and that gravy is the best I have ever had. Say, Gregory, save some more for me too. Pass those potatoes this way. And that gravy, too, Jenny, if you don't mind."

Grace shifted in her chair and dabbed her mouth with her napkin. She was still blushing at the compliments, but the sparkle in her eyes and the smile behind the napkin belied the fact that she was basking in the glow of their sentiments. It was good to see her this way.

Grace excused herself from the table and made her way to the kitchen. Jenny picked up some empty dishes and followed her mother. "Jenny, good, I'm glad you came in. Would you turn on the coffeemaker while I cut the pie?"

"Sure, Mom. Do you think they will really have any room for dessert out there?"

"I would rather see a guest enjoy his food and come back for seconds than to have him just move it around on his plate," Grace said and smiled. She turned back to the fresh apple pie and cut it into generous portions. "Besides, Pastor Tom probably doesn't get a lot of home cooking. Someday he will make some woman a fine husband."

"Why, because he likes to eat home cooking? That just sounds like a lot of work for the poor woman who marries him," Jenny said with a laugh. "I'll go see what I can clear off the table to make room for that pie."

Gregory and Pastor Tom had pushed their plates away and were engaged in a lively conversation when Jenny came back into the room. Scooping up the dishes, she said, "I hope you both saved room for Mom's apple pie. It looks delicious."

"If it's anything like the rest of the dinner, it will be," Pastor Tom exclaimed, patting his stomach. "I only hope I don't burst! All I can say is that it is a good thing I don't have to preach after this meal."

"Speaking of preaching, Pastor, why don't we have services on Sunday evenings anymore?" Jenny's dad asked. "I thought we only stopped them temporarily last winter, when the weather was so bad. Why didn't we pick them back up when spring arrived?"

Knowing this could become a heated discussion, Jenny quietly took her armful of dishes and retreated to the kitchen.

"Are they ready for dessert?" Grace asked as Jenny placed the dishes on the kitchen counter and began to scrape the plates.

"I think we have time to load the dishwasher. Dad just asked about Sunday evening services again."

Grace cringed. "I think you are right. You rinse and I'll load. We'll give them a few minutes to move on to another subject. Besides, it will give their dinner a little time to settle before dessert."

Harborview Community Church was a small church by almost anyone's standards. The attendance averaged around thirty-five on a Sunday morning. Of those who regularly attended Sunday mornings, only about fifteen also regularly attended the seven o'clock service on Sunday evenings. Last winter the weather had been so bad so often that the church members decided to temporarily suspend the evening worship services until the weather became more conducive to travel. For some reason, however, when spring arrived, bringing the good weather with it, the services had not been reinstated. Pastor Tom had never pushed to start the Sunday evening services back up again, and some of the regulars were a little disappointed with his procrastination. The discussion had taken place many times. And it always seemed to end at the same stalemate.

"You know, Gregory," Pastor Tom said as Jenny came into the dining room for another load of dirty dishes, "the weather is already turning cold. There would be no sense in starting up the evening services again now. We would probably only have to stop them again once the snow starts flying."

"Well, you may be right about the weather, but I am not convinced about the services," countered Gregory. "Last year was not a normal year for snow. We usually don't get that much. We didn't have to cancel all the services the winter before last. Or any winter that I can remember for that matter. Couldn't we have the services and come up with a severe weather cancellation plan? We could do a call list or something. There's only a handful of us."

"That's my point exactly. The ones who come to the evening services are the ones who come to everything. They are the ones who are involved in worship services and prayer meetings and Bible studies and committee meetings and—"

"So are you saying we don't need the evening worship service because we get enough already?" Gregory interrupted. "I just can't see the logic in that," he added, a little louder than usual. "Does there actually come a point in the week when we get too much worship time? Are you trying to tell me that, Pastor?"

Jenny perceived a slight sneer in her father's voice. It was very unusual for her even-tempered dad and a definite sign that it was time for the dessert to come out.

"Mom, we need the dessert out there now," Jenny said as she set down the last of the dishes from the table. "We need to save Dad before he says more that he wants to about Sunday nights."

"Oh, dear," Grace said and moaned. "Here, take the pie. I'll be right behind you with the coffee tray."

"Dessert is served," Jenny announced with a flourish as she worked her way between her father's chair and the preacher's chair. They had moved their chairs slightly to face one another during their conversation, and Jenny was deliberately trying to focus their concentration elsewhere. Instinctively, both scooted their chairs back up to the table, Gregory at the head and the pastor on one side. *Good boys*, Jenny thought as she dished the pie up on the china dessert plates and carefully laid a wedge of cheddar cheese on each plate. Grace always served cheese with pie, as had her mother before her. It was supposed to take the sweet taste out of one's mouth after eating the pie. Jenny handed a plate to Pastor Tom and watched for a reaction. Some people looked puzzled at the cheese but didn't say anything. Others would ask about it outright. In Jenny's world, it had always been there, but she was discovering more and more that people were unaware of the custom, so it had become a game for her to try to guess people's responses. She guessed the pastor would just get a puzzled look.

"Hmmm, what's this?" Pastor Tom asked as he picked up the cheese and nibbled on the end.

*So much for being a good judge of people's reactions,* Jenny thought with a smile.

"It's to cleanse the palate after the dessert," Grace explained as she poured coffee from the other side of the table. "Would you care for cream in your coffee, Pastor?"

"No, thank you, Grace," the pastor replied politely. "You sure have served a wonderful dinner today, and this pie will be the perfect ending to a perfect meal. Thank you for inviting me to dinner. It has truly been my pleasure to have shared it with you." Turning to Jenny, he added, "Jenny, when you get married, if you cook only half as well as your mother, your husband will never want to leave your table!"

"Well, then," Jenny said tongue in cheek, "I had better never get married. We would be poor quickly if he only wanted to eat and never go out to work."

"I guess you're right about that, Jenny," the pastor said with a laugh. "Who would buy the groceries?"

The look on Jenny's face brought another round of laughter to the table. The conversation about the church services was soon forgotten in the revelry of good food, good company, and laughter.

CHAPTER

8

Jenny's eyes opened quickly. She was fully awake in an instant. There was no rolling over and stretching to wake up this morning. There was no basking in the stream of sunlight that filtered through her lace curtains, making spider web patterns on her quilt, before she put feet to floor. There was no contemplating the day ahead as she decided whether to shower first or spend time in the Word of God. She was just suddenly wide-awake. And it was strange.

Jenny listened. Had someone called her? Had an unfamiliar noise startled her awake? As she strained to hear, she heard only the beating of her heart. It had not been racing when she awoke, but as she tried to figure out why she had awakened so vividly, she could feel her pulse rate increase. In the stillness of the morning, she tried to make sense of the whole thing.

As Jenny lay in her bed, in the comfort of her own room, she began to remember. She had been dreaming again, but this time it was different. This time there was no pain, no tears, no thrashing about in her bed. This time there was no accident, no forgetfulness, no frustration. Yet at the same time, it dawned on her that it had not been so much a dream but a remembrance. It was more like reliving something that had actually taken place—something she had not remembered until just now.

"Oh, Lord, help me to remember," Jenny passionately, imploringly whispered. But it was gone. That which she tried so hard to remember about the "dream" felt like sand falling through her fingers. The dream had been right there in her hand, but the more she struggled to remember it—to hold on to it—the more her fingers opened, allowing it to flow through.

"Why God, why did You allow me a little piece and then take it away?" Jenny again whispered as the tears welled in her eyes. She closed her eyes and sighed. And in that sigh, her Lord spoke to her heart, telling Jenny to *Relax and Listen.*

Once again, Jenny's eyes opened with a start. Had she imagined what she just heard? Could it really have been that still, small voice of God? A strange phenomenon to say the least. But Jenny did not feel startled at the sound. In fact, she felt quite the opposite. Jenny felt as though a blanket of comfort covered her. Her pulse rate returned to normal, and she could feel herself relaxing as she lay against the pillow. The sunlight once again made lacy patterns on her quilt, and as she focused on them, her eyelids grew heavy, and Jenny slipped into a peaceful sleep.

The snow was falling softly, and in the twilight of the early evening, the flakes looked like tiny shimmering stars all around them. The streetlights encompassing the square just added to the sparkle of the newly fallen snow still unmarred by footprints. They could have chosen to sit in the gazebo and watch the snow fall from inside the protective shelter, but they chose one of the small wrought iron benches placed in a circular fashion around the outside of the gazebo. In the spring, they had sat together on this very same bench and watched a band play in the gazebo. In the spring, they had listened as the band played show tunes to the crowd in the square. In the spring, they had laughed as they watched children dancing to the music. But it was winter now. Months had passed since they laughed together on the bench. Now they sat together in quiet contemplation. Jenny shivered, and Ben placed his arm around her shoulders and drew her closer. She looked down and saw his hand draped over her shoulder. He was wearing the leather gloves she had given him for Christmas. With his hand that close to her face, she could smell the still-new smell of the leather.

"Jenny," Ben whispered, "I have to go away."

Once more Jenny opened her eyes in the stillness of her room. Once more she looked around at familiar surroundings. This time she was calm as she remembered the dream. She had recognized the gazebo and the bench. She could see the band playing from that long ago spring. She even remembered the feel of the snow falling on her face. But try as she might, she still could not see Ben's face.

*If only I could have dreamed a little longer*, she thought. *If only I had looked up into his face*, she reprimanded herself. *If only, if only …*

Getting out of bed, Jenny knelt beside it and prayed,

> Father, God, thank You so much for speaking to me today. Thank You for Your comfort and for Your grace. Thank You for the piece of my past You have let me remember this morning. But Lord, I am still confused. Why can't I remember more than that? Why do I remember the gazebo but not the man I sat with on the bench? How can I remember the spring and the band and the children and not remember the person who shared those things with me? How is it that I even remember buying the gloves as a Christmas present but still cannot put a face to the man I gave them to. It doesn't make any sense to me at all.
>
> Father, I know that You want me to remember these things. I am even more sure of that now, after this morning. That gazebo is near the college. Am I supposed to go back to Montague? You know I have been thinking about that already. Is this Your way of telling me that it is where I need to be?
>
> Father, You are in control of all things. Help me to rest in that reality. I will tell Mom and Dad today that I want to move out and go back to Montague. Please prepare their hearts to hear this news.
>
> I feel like You have led me on the first step of a journey. Help me not to get lost on the way. Keep me strong. In Jesus's name, Amen.

Jenny did not get up right away but remained by her bed. She shifted from the kneeling position to a more comfortable reclining position against her bed. The room was quiet. *What did I expect, a two-way conversation? Did I expect God to open His mouth and speak to me out loud, right here, right now?*

A soft knock on her door brought Jenny back into focus. "Come in," she said.

As Grace opened the door, she said, "Jenny, honey, we are getting ready to sit down to breakfast. I am making pancakes. Do you want to join us?" Stepping further into the room, Grace saw Jenny on the floor beside her bed. "Are you OK, Jenny? Why are you on the floor?"

"I was praying and just felt like kneeling by the bed," Jenny responded matter-of-factly. She surprised herself at how calm she sounded. "Mom," she began, "I've been thinking about getting back out on my own. Think Dad would mind if I went to Montague and stayed at the apartment? Maybe I could get a job at the college again. They would probably hire me back in the library, don't you think?"

Grace took a step backwards without even thinking. She grabbed the bedroom door for support. She was visibly shaken but fought for control. "Jenny," she said with a quiver in her voice, "do you think you are ready, honey? Why do you want to leave? Why not just stay here? Don't you like working for the school here? What is there in Montague for you? What will you do on the days that Dad doesn't stay over?"

The more Grace spoke, the less control she maintained. The color had drained from her face. Jenny got up and walked over to her mother. "Oh, Mom," she said, "I'll be OK. I am grown up now you know. And I *have* lived away from home before. I just think it is time to get back out there and on my own a little bit. I can't live at home forever. Besides, Dad will be there part of the time, so I really won't be completely on my own now, will I?" She wrapped her arms around her trembling mother and smiled. "Now, what about those pancakes? I'm starving. How about if you get them on the griddle, and I will be right down?"

CHAPTER

9

G regory Peterson was sitting in the breakfast nook with another cup of coffee growing cold on the table, his face again hidden behind the newspaper. It was typical Gregory. It was how Grace and Jenny expected to find him when they entered the kitchen in the morning. Grace had been sitting there with him just a few minutes before, sipping her coffee and leafing through the latest recipe magazine. It had been a morning like every other morning when Gregory was home. Gregory and Grace had always been early risers, but Gregory usually managed to make it to the kitchen first in the morning. The coffeepot was always prepared the night before, and he simply turned it on as he went through the kitchen on his way outside to pick up the morning paper. By the time Grace came into the kitchen, Gregory had assumed his position. Grace would get herself a cup of coffee and join him at the little table, picking up whatever section of the paper Gregory had finished reading or perhaps the latest magazine. By the time they were ready for breakfast, they were pretty much both wide-awake and caught up on the happenings of the world.

Jenny, on the other hand, usually stayed in her room for a bit in the mornings. She had developed a habit of spending time in the Word of God and praying before starting her day. She had also started keeping a journal after the accident since someone had told her that writing things down might help her remember. At first it had been exciting to write things down as they came back to her. But soon, Jenny came to the conclusion that her memory had never really been gone. It was all in there, each memory still intact, just needing a nudge to reappear. Although she diligently wrote down each remembrance as it was nudged out of her dormant memory, the excitement was soon replaced by frustration. Thoughts of the mysterious Ben soon plagued the pages of her journal, and the excitement of memories renewed were replaced with the frustration of memories she could not yet grasp. Her journal became a combination of diary and prayer journal. Each piece of information she could formulate about Ben was meticulously recorded in it and usually followed by a heart's cry to her Lord for understanding and direction. She often wondered how she would stand it at all without her faith in Christ. She begged the Father to help her remember or to take away the desire to know altogether. Yet she remained tortured by partial memories and a longing to put them all together. In her faith, she knew she must trust all to the One who loved her most, but sometimes the practice of her faith was a challenge. It was with this thought in mind that Jenny decided to go down to breakfast and keep the journaling until later in the day, after she had time to process the morning's dream.

Jenny came down the stairs, not to the smell of pancakes, not to finding her dad behind the newspaper and oblivious to his surroundings, not to finding her mom standing at the stove, but instead to catching a glimpse of her mom and dad huddled at the table, heads close together, and obviously in an intense discussion. Jenny hesitated. Should she enter the kitchen and interrupt them or slip quietly back upstairs. She could guess the topic of discussion. As it turned out, she didn't have time to make a decision as her dad looked up at that moment and wished her a good morning.

"Good morning," said Jenny. "I think," she added under her breath as her mom scurried over to the counter and began to mix the pancake batter. Gregory did not lift his newspaper back up but instead looked at Jenny and said matter-of-factly, "Mom tells me you are thinking about going back to Montague with me."

Jenny smiled. "I am. Actually, I have been thinking about it for a while now. I think it is time I spread my wings and spend some time out in the real world."

"And we do not live in the real world here?" Gregory asked, raising a quizzical eyebrow.

Jenny laughed. "You know what I mean, Dad."

"Yea, I know," he said. "But your mom is a little concerned that you are not ready yet."

"Not ready yet? How can I not be ready yet? I already lived out on my own when I went to Montague. You didn't worry about me then," Jenny said in an exasperated tone. "I *am* a grown woman."

"You are right. You are a grown woman. But to us, Jenny, you will always be our little girl, and we worry about you. Do you feel strong enough to go back to work on a regular schedule?" her dad quizzed her.

"Dad," Jenny said, trying to keep an even tone, "I have been working right here in Harborview, and I have survived. In fact, I get called in to work at a moment's notice. I go to my job totally unprepared for the day ahead. And I rarely go to the same place twice. Do you know what it is like to be the substitute teacher for elementary and junior high kids? If I can face that challenge, surely I can handle working in a quiet college library on a regular basis. That is, of course, if there is an opening there, and if they will take me back. It *has* been almost two years now."

"OK, I get the point. I guess your mom and I never thought of your job here in quite that way. Getting called in at the last moment to face those kids would be enough of a challenge for me, let alone actually spending the whole day with them. Yes, point well taken, Jenny. I guess we can't argue with that."

Gregory picked up the paper once again and retreated to the safety offered behind its pages. Jenny glanced at her mom and caught the look on her face before she turned back to the pancake batter. The look would have told Gregory that she couldn't believe he had given in so easily, but Gregory had missed the look and thus the message behind it. The moment had passed, but Jenny was confident her mom would make another attempt at the dissuasion before Jenny was actually on her way to Montague.

Jenny did not have to wait long for her mom to make her next move.

CHAPTER

# 10

"Jenny, Jenny, honey. The phone is for you," Grace called up the stairs. *Funny,* Jenny thought, *I didn't hear the phone ring.* "OK, Mom. I'll get it up here," Jenny called back down the stairs.

"Hello," Jenny said. As she spoke, she heard the click of the downstairs phone being hung up.

"Hello, Jenny. It's Mary Worthington over at Killary's?" Mary spoke the words in a voice that was more a question than a statement. Jenny smiled as she wondered if Mary was introducing herself or just wondering who she was or perhaps from where she was calling. Jenny remembered Mary as one of the ladies in Grace's Sunday school class and women's group. She worked in the women's department at the store. In fact, she was working the day Jenny bought her new red sweater.

"Yes, Mrs. Worthington. What a nice surprise. What can I do for you?"

"Jenny, your mom mentioned that you were going to look for a regular job, and I just heard that the store was hiring, so I thought I would call and let you know. It really is a nice place to work. I've been there twelve years myself."

Not wanting to hurt poor Mary's feelings, Jenny said, "Oh, Mrs. Worthington, if I worked at the store, I would spend my whole paycheck on new clothes before I ever got it to the bank! But thank you for calling to let me know about the opening. I will definitely keep the opportunity in mind."

"Well, OK, Jenny. We would love to have you at Killary's. I'm sure they would hire you right away," Mary tried one more time.

"Thank you again for calling. I will definitely think about it. You have a nice day, OK? Bye, now."

"Goodbye," Mary said with a sigh in her voice.

Jenny couldn't help but chuckle as she replaced the phone. She could definitely see Grace's hand in *that* phone call. By the time Jenny got downstairs, Grace was gone. There was a note on the counter:

Jenny—
Went to run a few errands. I will stop at the church and drop the books off for the library. I should be home about 4:00.

Love,
Mom

"Well, she got out of that one, didn't she?" But since Mom brought up the job hunt, no time like the present to give Montague a call and see if they needed any good library help.

Jenny went into the family room, picked up the phone, and began to dial the old, familiar number for the library at Montague. *Another thing I remember*, she thought mid-dial. She used to think it was odd that she would remember certain non-important things, but the things that really mattered eluded her so easily. Except for the memory of Ben. Or maybe she should say the lack thereof. She had to put that kind of thinking behind her now. The faith she maintained did not allow for coincidences and such. God was sovereign, and she had surrendered to the fact that He knew best how to heal her of her amnesia. Maybe God had a sense of humor. She recalled having once remembered an old boyfriend's high school locker combination while not being able to remember her own birthday. Jenny had been devastated at the time, but those things were in the past and now only humorous stories. Still, she recalled, she was on a new mission, and that mission included getting out of Harborview and continuing her quest to find the one and only thing that still eluded her memory—Ben. Coming back to her senses, Jenny realized she had been standing there with the phone in her hand. The dial tone had long since ceased to sound. She had to hang up and begin again to complete her task.

*Rinngggg ... Rinngggg ... Rinngggg ... click*!

"Hello, Montague University Library. This is Steve. How may I help you?" answered a rich tenor voice.

"Hello, Steve. My name is Jenny Peterson. I was wondering if Mr. Swenson was available," Jenny replied.

"Yes, I believe he is in his office. Let me check and see if he is available," Steve replied rather professionally.

Jenny giggled as she waited. It was only a few seconds before she heard Mr. Swenson's familiar voice. "Jenny? Jenny Peterson? Is that really you?"

"Yes, Mr. Swenson. It is really me. How are you?" Jenny asked with a smile in her voice. Mr. Swenson had not only been a terrific boss but one of her favorite people at Montague. Maybe it had something to do with his position at the library. She was as fond of him as she was of Carleton here in the library at Harborview. Maybe she just had a thing for librarians. It is amazing the thoughts that can run through one's mind in a split second, during a momentary pause in conversation.

Mr. Swenson's reply jolted her back to the conversation at hand. "Well, Jenny, I am as good as my body will let me be these days. But more importantly, how are you?" he asked, sympathy oozing into his tone of voice.

"I am fine but getting a little restless around here. In fact, that is why I was calling. I am thinking about moving back to Montague, and I was hoping to find a job on campus. I don't suppose there are any openings in the library, are there?" Jenny asked in a hopeful voice.

"Well, Jenny, as a matter of fact, the student who was doing your job graduated in June. She did work through the summer but has moved on this fall, and I have not found a replacement yet. I would love to have you back here in the library." He paused.

Jenny could tell he had something else on his mind. "What is it, Mr. Swenson? Do you have someone else in mind? I don't want you to feel obligated to offer me the position if you are considering someone else. It wasn't fair of me to call and ask like this. I'm sorry if I have put you in an awkward position. Maybe I should have just called human resources and asked what kind of openings they had. Maybe I will do that. OK?" Jenny knew she was rambling, but she had not even thought about that before she called.

"Wait a minute, Jenny," Mr. Swenson interrupted. "Not so fast there, girl. I do not have anyone else in mind for the position, and I am glad you called. I was just surprised and wondering if you were up to the move and the job. Your dad has been keeping me posted on your progress since the accident, and he had not mentioned that you were considering such a move. I thought you were still recovering at home."

"Oh, is that it?" Her jaw muscles had tightened. Did her folks think she was really such an invalid? "I assure you, Mr. Swenson, that I have fully recovered. In fact, I have been working here as a substitute teacher for over a year now. I think I can fully function in my old position there in the library. That is," she paused and with a softness in her voice added, "if you will still have me."

"Well, my girl, consider yourself had," he exclaimed. "I will be looking forward to having you back. When do you suppose you can start?"

"You know, I hadn't thought that far ahead. But I can come back to Montague this weekend and be all settled in when Dad drives back in on Tuesday. I'm going to stay at the apartment there. At least for a while."

"Good! Then it's all settled. Come in and see me as soon as you get settled in, and we'll talk more."

"Thanks, Mr. Swenson. I look forward to seeing you."

"And I you. OK. Drive safely, Jenny, and I'll see you soon. Goodbye."

"Goodbye, Mr. Swenson. And thanks again."

Jenny smiled as she put down the phone. *Well, it's settled then. I am on my way out of Harborview and back into the world of Montague. I wonder what will happen there.* She looked down at the phone she had just hung up and let out a deep sigh. She was not sure what lay ahead, but she was convinced this was the path she needed to take. It just felt right.

CHAPTER

# 11

J enny was just finishing up sorting through her closet when she heard her mom come in the front door downstairs. *Hmmmm ... must be four o'clock already,* she thought as she shut the closet door. There was a pile of clothes on her bed and another pile on her chair. One pile was to go with her; the other was to be given away. Summer things still hung in the closet, but there would be plenty of time to come back for them before summer came.

"Jenny, I'm home," Grace called from the bottom of the stairs. "Are you up there?"

"Hi, Mom," Jenny said as she made her way down the stairs. "How are things at the church library?"

"Oh, the library is fine. I got all the books put away and had time to dust all the shelves while I was there. Someone donated a whole bag of books. They left them by the door to the library. I brought them home to sort through. I left the bag by the front door if you want to look them over and see if there is anything you would like to read," Grace rambled on as she hung up her coat. She tended to do that when she was trying to avoid a conversation. Jenny knew that Grace was waiting for her to mention the phone call from Mary Worthington. It may have been kinder just to mention it and move on, but Jenny only played along, not bringing up the call at all. She thought she would let her mom squirm a little bit more before letting her off the hook.

An awkward silence followed. Jenny smiled. This was way too much fun—if not a little bit sadistic. Poor Grace.

"I saw a man and woman in the pastor's office when I was at the church. They were just coming out when I was getting ready to leave. I stopped by the office to say goodbye to Irene, and do you know what she told me?" Grace asked, seemingly trying to make any conversation at all so Jenny would not ask her about Mary's call.

"No, Mom, but knowing Irene, it was probably some hot little bit of gossip that she should have kept to herself. I don't know why Pastor Tom keeps her on in the church office if she cannot learn to be more discreet," Jenny replied. Grace got all the latest gossip from Irene at the church, but she usually had the common sense not to repeat it—at least not until she had checked it out for herself to see if it were true. After all, it really wasn't gossip if it were the truth, was it?

"Well, she told me the couple in the office with the pastor were there asking about church membership," Grace said with a bit of disdain in her voice.

"So? What is so bad about that? We could use some more members in the church."

"But Jenny, they were ... they were Mexicans," she whispered with a little hiss in her voice. "Can you imagine that? Mexicans wanting to come to *our* church. Pretty soon they will bring in a whole bunch of them, and we will be overrun. The church will never be the same again. You know how *they* are."

Jenny raised her eyebrows a bit and gave her mother an incredulous look that told Grace Jenny could not believe she had actually heard her mother say such things. "What do you mean, Mom? What does it matter if they are Mexicans? They are people. People who either need the Lord or people who have found the Lord and want to worship with other believers. Either way, their nationality does not factor into the equation."

Grace looked at Jenny as if now *she* couldn't believe what she was hearing. Then Grace's expression changed altogether. It became a look of resignation. It was almost as if she had expected Jenny to react that way and yet hoped she would not. *Very strange,* thought Jenny, *what kind of a look was that?*

Before Jenny had a chance to question the fleeting look, Grace continued in a much more subdued tone, "Irene said the couple had heard about the church from that homeless shelter Mary and I took the sweaters to last month."

"But wouldn't that be a good thing? Don't we want the people we minister to react in a positive way? Isn't that *why* we minister to them?" Jenny replied with a hint of sarcasm.

"Yes," Grace stated. "But we don't need them to react by coming to *our* church. They need to stay with their own kind. They can worship much better in a church with people like themselves."

Jenny couldn't believe what she was hearing! Her perfect, godly little mother—the one she strove to be like, the person who would do anything for anyone—was prejudiced! She had been sorting clothes and collecting toiletry items to take to the homeless shelter for as long as Jenny could remember. And all that time, she had been prejudiced! It didn't make any sense.

"Mom, that's just pure prejudice! How can you do the things you do for the homeless shelter and then act this way when the ministry shows the fruit of your efforts?"

"I am *not* prejudiced!" Grace responded, appalled at the thought. "How can you say that, Jenny?"

"How can I say that?" Jenny almost laughed. "How can I say that? Just listen to yourself. You just told me that this couple had no business at our church because they are Mexican. I still can't believe you actually said it. But if *that* is not prejudice, then I don't know what is!"

"It's not prejudice, Jenny. It's simple fact. People need to stay with their own kind, that's all. After all, a church full of Mexicans would not want us to come and be part of *their* church, would they?"

Jenny could tell from her mother's explanation and tone of voice that she actually believed what she was saying. Grace actually thought there were "kinds" of people, and that people should stick with their own kind.

"But I don't understand, Mom. Why do you and your women's group minister to the people at the homeless shelter? Why do you take canned food there and toiletries and sweaters? Why do you wash and mend clothes and sew buttons on coats to take them there? It doesn't make any sense. I never thought of you as a hypocrite before."

Grace's countenance fell. It was like Jenny had slapped her hard. She had never been able to explain it to Jenny. This conversation had an all-too-familiar ring to it, yet to Jenny, it seemed like a brand-new revelation.

"Jenny," Grace said and paused. It was as though she was mustering her strength for a battle. Or perhaps Jenny had just gone a little bit too far when she insinuated that Grace was a hypocrite. Jenny already regretted her own words. "Jenny," Grace began again. This time her voice was soft. "God calls us to love our neighbor as we love ourselves. He teaches us to minister to the less fortunate. However, God does not mean for us to mingle in our everyday lives. We can minister to people. We can love them. We can lead them to Christ. We can even help them to get their own church up and running so they can worship together. But He does not call us to take them out of their own worlds and plop them into ours. It is just not right."

Jenny's jaw fell. She had to consciously make the effort to close her mouth. Her mom actually believed that what she was saying was the gospel truth. Her mom's heart was toward God and the ministry to which God calls all Christians, but her thoughts on this were just plain convoluted. Where did this idea come from? Pastor Tom had certainly never preached this from the pulpit. She had never heard it in a Sunday school class. Where did this come from, and how could her mom possibly buy into this idea?

"Mom, that doesn't make any sense."

Grace was not ready for another philosophical discussion about this. "Jenny," she said, determined to end this particular conversation, "we have had this discussion many times before, and we agreed to just disagree agreeably on this one. Why are you making an issue of it again? I am sorry I mentioned the couple at church at all." *It would have been easier if I had just asked her if she took the job at Killary's* Grace thought. "I'm going to go see about getting dinner started," said Grace as she headed for the kitchen.

Jenny was left standing at the bottom of the stairs, watching her mother walk away. She was speechless. Dropping to sit on the bottom step, Jenny replayed the conversation in her mind. One thing her mother said kept tumbling over and over: *"We have had this discussion many times before. Why are you making an issue of it again?"* Jenny couldn't remember ever having had this conversation before. Surely this was one subject she would remember talking about. Even more so, this should have been one thing she would have remembered about her mom.

A few months ago, this would have been just one more thing she did not remember. But she had come to a place where she was convinced that she had remembered everything. Her memory was intact now. It was all there except the elusive memories associated with Ben. Those memories, she was convinced, were the only ones left to unlock. Those memories were the purpose of her quest. Arriving at this point had allowed her to summon the courage to go out and search for this one remaining empty spot from her past. But now she wondered if maybe there were more memories hidden away in the deepest recesses of her psyche. The reminder from her mother about having this discussion many times before really knocked Jenny for a loop. Perhaps her parents were correct. Perhaps she wasn't over her amnesia after all. Perhaps she really wasn't ready to venture outside of Harborview and away from the safety of her family and her home. Perhaps moving out was a foolish notion. Suppose Ben was only one of *many* things she had yet to remember. If so, then maybe concentrating all her efforts on recalling this one memory was only one small step in a long line of quests. She did not think she was up to an uphill battle. She turned her focus to God and prayed silently,

Lord, I don't understand. Have I misinterpreted Your leading? Have I wanted to remember this one thing so much that I refused to see the other things I have blocked out? Are there more memories yet to be discovered besides those concerning Ben? If so, I am not sure I am up to the fight. I am tired, Lord. I am tired before I even begin this fight, and I am not sure it is worth the effort. If I go and find my memories of Ben, will I have to do it all over again for some other memory? Will I have to do this for the rest of my life? You have brought me so far. I have remembered so much. Will You make me struggle for the rest of my memories?

I thought I had this all figured out. I thought You had answered my prayers and restored my memory. I asked You to help me remember Ben or to take the desire away completely. I trusted You.

Lord, I can work though this one search for lost memories as long as You are with me, but I don't have the strength to do it over and over. I don't have the strength to go through more dreams and more bits and pieces of memories. I just cannot do it.

As Jenny poured out her heart to the One she could always count on to hear, she could hear Him telling her that she indeed could not. The Lord had told her no but assured her of His promises. He reminded her that His strength was made perfect in her weaknesses. He called her His beloved child and reminded her of His promises to open when she knocked, show when she sought, and give when she asked. And then He assured her heart that He had not changed.

Jenny sat straight up! Did she really hear what she thought she heard? Was that the same still, small voice of God speaking again to her heart? It sounded almost like the voice spoke out loud it was so real. And yet, she had heard God speak to her before, just a few days ago in the stillness of her room. Maybe she had unconsciously passed that off as part of her dream, but she was not in her bed. Nor was she asleep this time. With a few self-controlled breaths, Jenny's heart rate returned to normal, and she smiled. Her God had never failed her. She trusted Him and would not stop now.

"Thank You, Lord," she whispered.

C H A P T E R

# 12

The ride to Montague took about two hours. It was a pleasant ride but could be treacherous in the winter. Gregory Peterson had been teaching at the university for a long time. He had worked on his doctorate degree while on staff at Montague University. Early on, when he was teaching full time, Gregory had secured the apartment close to the school. Sometimes, especially during the winter months, he stayed in Montague all week and only came home on weekends. He often wondered why he had not moved his family closer to the school. It would have saved a lot of driving time! But he always knew that the Peterson family were country folk at heart and could never bear giving up rural life for the convenience of the big city. Back then, Grace had a job she loved in Harborview, and the kids had lots of friends. Besides, the schools in Harborview were not only terrific scholastically, but because of their small size, every kid got the one-on-one attention they deserved. That was definitely important in the mind of an educator, and Gregory was definitely an educator.

As soon as he gained tenure at the university, though, Gregory arranged his teaching schedule to be able to spend more time at home. Since Grace retired, Gregory kept talking about retiring himself. But his love for teaching kept him from giving up his position completely. He had, however, limited himself to only teaching Tuesday/Thursday classes the last few semesters, and that schedule was working out well. He would drive to school on Tuesday mornings and stay over until classes were over on Thursday afternoons. If he left right after his last class on Thursday, he could usually make it back to Harborview in time to share a late dinner with his family. He held office hours on Wednesday and even taught a Wednesday evening class if enough students signed up. Gregory's schedule had enough classes to satisfy his desire to be in the classroom, imparting his vast knowledge to his students, while at the same time, allowing him some perks of semi-retirement. It also afforded him quite a lot of time to spend with Grace—while at the same time providing sufficient time apart so they didn't get on each other's nerves, which often happened when couples found themselves in each other's company all of the time. This arrangement was an ideal situation all the way around.

Gregory thought about Jenny as he drove. She had gone to college right after high school. She and Richard had both planned to go to Montague while they were growing up, but Jenny was the one who actually went. Richard joined the navy instead. He was four years older than Jenny and enlisted in the navy just as Jenny was beginning high school. Jenny always looked up to her big brother. She loved him very much, but there was just enough age difference between them to prevent them from traveling in the same social circles. While Richard was in high school, Jenny was still playing with her elementary-school friends. By the time Jenny went to high school, Richard was out in the world and deployed away from home. They had never gotten the chance to really become friends.

Richard married Beth while he was serving in the navy. He and Beth were stationed at the same place during the last year of Richard's service. They married in the chapel on the base and only moved back to this area when they had both finished their enlistment terms. They joined the reserves afterward and then settled in a home fifty miles from Montague about the time Jenny graduated from the university. Jenny had stayed on at the college and worked in the campus library after her graduation in June and had visited Richard and Beth a few times. She was enjoying getting to know both her brother and her new sister-in-law. In fact, she was driving home from their house the night of the accident.

Gregory was not one to think about Jenny's accident very often. He was much too practical. The accident happened, and Jenny came home to recuperate. End of subject. Her memory had returned, and there was no sense dwelling on the past. He was the kind of person who lived for the

FORGOTTEN MEMORIES SHATTERED DREAMS

present and neither relived the past nor longed for what tomorrow might bring. One of his favorite Bible verses came out of James 4:14: "for you do not know what tomorrow may bring."

Grace, on the other hand, worried a lot about what tomorrow might bring—especially when it came to Jenny, and even more after Ben had come into the picture. Gregory frowned as he remembered how upset Grace had gotten the first time she met Ben. She had come up to Montague with Gregory that week. Jenny was still living in the dorm, and they had planned some family time together at the apartment. Jenny had brought a friend to an early dinner on her parents' last afternoon at Montague. Gregory and Grace were leaving early that evening and had planned one last meal together with her before they left. Jenny's friend's name was Ben, and she was anxious for her parents to meet him. To say that the atmosphere became stiff soon after their arrival at the apartment would have been putting it mildly. The meal was over quickly, and Grace and Gregory left for Harborview as soon as the dishes were done. Gregory frowned again as he recalled the conversation that had monopolized their ride home. Grace was so worried that Jenny would get too close to this man. What if she actually developed feelings for him? How could she have actually befriended such a person in the first place? They had nothing in common. What on earth was Jenny thinking? Gregory recalled that Grace had raved and worried all the way home to Harborview—the *whole* two hours! By the time they arrived home, Grace had worked herself into such a frenzy that Gregory spent the next hour calming her down just so they could get some sleep.

Funny he should remember all that on this fine day. He wasn't taken to reminiscing. It must have something to do with Jenny's recent decision to move back to Montague. Deep down he knew the whole move had something to do with her lack of memories about Ben, although he had hoped she would let it all go when no one could fill in the blanks for her. Maybe he and Grace had been wrong to keep information from Jenny. Maybe if they had only answered her questions, she would have been satisfied and just dropped the whole thing. But what was done was done, and there was no sense dwelling on the what-ifs. And there was no sense in fearing the what-might-bes. They would just have to take it one day at a time now. If it all blew up in their faces, well, they would just have to deal with it then.

"Ah, Jenny, how nice to see you," Mr. Swenson exclaimed as Jenny was ushered into his office at the back of the library. Steve closed the door as he graciously backed out of the room. "Sit down, my dear girl. Sit down and make yourself comfortable." Mr. Swensen gestured toward the leather wing-backed chair across from his desk. Jenny loved his office, not because of the room itself, but more because of the way it felt. It was the perfect fit for one who loved books. It reminded her a little of the small library in Harborview, but only in atmosphere, not décor. This office was majestically ornate with big mahogany furniture. It had windows that went almost from the floor to the ceiling with heavy, burgundy, velvety drapes tied back with golden rope sashes. It was definitely a room that belonged in a well-established university. The bookcase behind Mr. Swenson's desk held volumes of the classics, but the effect was softened by the family pictures sitting in front of the books. The fact that Mr. Swenson loved books was evidenced all over his office. As many times as Jenny had been in this office, there was not one time she recalled seeing the top of his desk free from books. There were always a couple of them piled to one side and usually at least one lying open with a well-worn bookmark where the pages had most recently been lovingly caressed. Jenny smiled as she took a quick inventory and discovered that nothing had changed.

Settling herself in the chair, Jenny smiled back at Mr. Swenson. "I'm so glad there was an opening here. It's like coming home again."

"I know exactly how you feel. Having you back here is like welcoming family back from vacation. I was so glad you called when you did. A few days later, and the position might have been filled. I had been procrastinating about interviewing candidates, and you were an answer to prayer."

Once again Jenny heard the familiar Voice telling her that He loved her, His beloved one. He spoke to her heart, telling her that He had heard her prayers and the desires of her heart. That this was where she needed to be. And to just trust Him now and be patient.

"Thank You again, Lord," Jenny whispered.

Thinking she had only spoken in her heart, she realized she must have been more audible than she had anticipated because at that moment, Mr. Swenson looked up from some paperwork on his desk and said, "I'm sorry, Jenny. Did you say something?"

"No. Just thinking too loudly, I guess. I was just realizing how much this job was an answer to prayer for me as well. Isn't it amazing how the Lord works things out in exactly the way they need to be?"

And we know that all things work together for good, to those who love God, to those who are the called according to His purpose (Romans 8:28 NKJV).

Jenny smiled again. Just smiled and loved the Lord in her spirit.

All too soon, Mr. Swenson drew her back to the physical realm. "I guess if you just finish filling out your portion of these papers, we can see about getting you on the schedule. When would you like to start work, Jenny?"

"I am ready anytime. I came up over the weekend and have gotten myself settled into Dad's apartment. He is driving in this morning. Actually, he is probably already here and on his way to class. There's nothing left for me to do but to jump right in."

"Good. It's settled then," Mr. Swenson said, reaching for the intercom button on the phone. "Steve, could you come in here when you get a minute, please."

"Right away, sir," came the muffled response. In only a few seconds, there was a light rap on the door. Steve opened it just enough to stick his head and shoulder in and look expectantly at Mr. Swenson.

"Come on in, Steve," came the expected invitation. Steve entered, closing the door silently behind him, and approached the desk. Mr.

Swenson continued, "Jenny has graciously consented to come back to work with us here at Montague. I don't believe you were here yet when she was last with us, but she was a very valuable asset to the library, and I expect she will be again. Would you take her paperwork when she is finished, and be sure it gets to Mrs. Clark in the personnel office? Also, would you show Jenny around and introduce her to anyone out there she does not already know?"

"Sure thing, Mr. Swenson," Steve replied enthusiastically. "Anything else I can do for you?"

"No, I think that will cover it for now. Thanks." Mr. Swenson stood, turned toward Jenny, and said, "Jenny, I am glad to have you here. Steve will show you around today, although I doubt anything has changed much. You can officially begin your workweek in the morning. I will be sure to add you to the schedule, and I will see you at nine o'clock. Any questions for me?"

Jenny reached to shake Mr. Swenson's hand. "No, not right now. Thank you again for giving me the job. I look forward to being back here."

Mr. Swenson gave Jenny's hand a squeeze. "Me too. I will leave you in Steve's capable hands now and will see you first thing in the morning." With a nod to Steve, Mr. Swenson returned to his chair, and Jenny turned to follow Steve out into the next phase of her adventure.

CHAPTER

# 14

regory's first class was not until eleven, but he made it a habit to arrive at his office well in advance of class time. He had a set routine of checking his mail and organizing the day ahead as soon as he arrived. This trip to Montague was no exception. However, soon after he began his ritual, there was a knock on his door.

"Come in," Gregory said as he looked up. The door opened slowly, and a hand reached in holding a cup. Gregory could smell his favorite cappuccino and smiled. "Mmmm, French vanilla." He sighed. Jenny popped her head around the door, and her smile met his.

"Hope you have time for a cup before class, Dad," Jenny said as she made her way across the small office, handed the cup to her father, and sat down in the dark-green padded chair facing her dad's desk.

Gregory closed his calendar and grade book to give Jenny his full attention. "From the smile on your face, can I assume things are falling into place for you here?" It was just like Dad to think of the practical aspect of her visit.

"Yes. I am settled in at the apartment. I saw Mr. Swenson this morning, and I report for work at the library tomorrow morning. Oh, Dad, it felt so good to be back in the library. And so … right. It's like this is where I am supposed to be right now."

"That's great, honey. You know, your mom will miss you terribly."

"I know, Dad. But I really think it's time. I can't live at home forever."

Gregory did not offer any further comment, but the silence that followed was not uncomfortable. Each sat sipping cappuccino and relaxing. Jenny thought how very much her parents complemented one another. Here was her dad, practical and comfortable with the quiet. Her mom, on the other hand, was emotional and would have had to fill the silence with something … anything. The thought brought a smile to Jenny's face, and her father, watching her, lifted an eyebrow. "Something amusing?"

"No, I was just thinking of Mom and how she would have had to say or do something to break the silence in this room. It would have driven her nuts!"

Gregory smiled. Looking at his watch, he said, "Well, I hate to break up this little Kodak moment, but I need to get to class. I just hate it when the professor is late." He rose, dropped the Styrofoam cup in the trash can, and leaned over to kiss Jenny on the top of her head as he headed for the door. "Thanks for the cappuccino. It was delicious. Be sure to lock the door on your way out, will you, sweetheart?"

"Sure, Dad. By the way, what time will you get home tonight? I'll cook dinner," Jenny offered as she turned in her chair to watch him leave. "Any requests?"

"I'll be home about 6:30. Surprise me." The last part of the comment was muffled as Gregory closed the door and was off to class. Jenny took another sip of the cappuccino and glanced around the small office. She had not been in there for a couple of years now. The room was a far cry from Mr. Swenson's ornate office, but it served its purpose. Gregory had been fortunate to secure an office with a window, even if the view from that window was over the east parking lot. At least it afforded a bit of sunlight, especially in the early morning hours. The sun was shining in the window, and the shaft of light made little dust particles dance in its stream.

Jenny rose from the chair and walked around behind her father's desk. There was just enough room behind the desk for a narrow bookcase and a tall file cabinet. Pictures of the Petersons were proudly displayed atop the file cabinet. There was one of Jenny in her cap and gown with the main hall of Montague as a backdrop. There was a picture of Richard in his naval uniform. There was a picture of Richard and Beth on their wedding day. There was a picture of Gregory and Grace together. But it was the picture of the whole family that brought a special smile to Jenny's face. As she picked it up for a closer look, she was reminded of the day it was taken. The five of them had gone for a family portrait. They had all dressed up and gone to the photographer's only to discover that they were a day late for their appointment. There they were, all dressed up and nowhere to go. Grace was flustered and not convinced that the fault lay with her. Richard was just quiet. Beth, being quite new to the family, did not know how to react. Jenny recalled trying to reassure her mom that it was not a big deal. And Gregory—practical Dad—said, "So let's do something special today. It seems a shame to waste all this finery on a Saturday afternoon. How about dinner and a show?"

Grace looked up from her distress and gave Gregory a hopeful look. Richard, following in his father's practical footsteps, pointed out the fact that there were no fancy restaurants or shows in Harborview.

"Oh, really?" Gregory countered. "Well, I happen to know where the very best dining is in this whole county! You just wait and see if it is not the most beautiful place to eat you have been to in a long time."

Everyone turned to Gregory, fully expecting more elaboration. But he just put a finger to his lips and smiled. "Shhh, it will be a surprise. But I guarantee you will not be disappointed. Now, everyone to the car!"

The mood lightened. Gregory hooked his arms in Grace's on one side and in Jenny's on the other. Richard shrugged, linked arms with Beth, and the two of them followed Gregory and his girls to the car.

Gregory hummed a tune as he drove and kept winking at Grace, who was finally beginning to smile. Beth sat in the back seat, between Richard and Jenny. Richard had his arm on the back of the seat, behind Beth's shoulders, but could not resist the temptation to tease his little sister. In typical older brother fashion, he kept tapping Jenny's shoulder and tickling her neck. Beth whispered for him to leave his sister alone, but Jenny just smiled and gave him a look that promised payback would come when he least expected it. Beth, being an only child, saw the playful looks Jenny and Richard exchanged but just looked from one to the other in utter confusion.

Gregory turned the car into the parking lot of the local grocery store and excused himself for a moment. He got out of the car and headed toward the store. Grace watched him make his way to the entrance, and once he disappeared inside, she turned in her seat to face the back-seaters.

She began to apologize again for getting them all dressed up and dragging them to the photography studio only to not be able to get the portrait done when they got there.

"It's OK, Mom," Richard said.

"It's really fine, Mrs. Peterson," Beth added. "There will be another opportunity."

"Thank you, Beth, but I really feel bad about the whole thing." She paused and then continued on a lighter note, "By the way, don't you think it is time you stopped calling me Mrs. Peterson? We want you to feel like part of the family, dear, even if we are a bit unorganized at times. I'm afraid you just don't know what you have signed on to be a part of." Grace reached back and patted Beth's hand.

A few minutes later, Gregory reappeared and walked to the back of the car. He stowed his purchases in the trunk and then came around to the driver's side and got in the car.

"Greg, what are you doing?" asked Grace. "What did you need in there? Did you buy something that will spoil before we get home? Where are we going anyway?"

"Now wife, relax. Everything is under control. We are about to embark on our family outing," Gregory replied with another wink. "Everyone ready?" he asked as he fastened his seat belt, put the car in gear, and eased out of the parking spot.

It did not take long to get to Gregory's destination. Just a few miles down the road, he steered the car into the park. Everyone in the car gave each other a quizzical look but knew that if they even asked the question, Gregory would not reveal his plans.

Parking the car, Gregory announced, "OK, we're here. Everyone out of the car."

"Dad, we're at the park," Richard offered in a matter-of-fact voice.

"On the contrary, my misinformed progeny. We are at God's Theater. The show for today will be 'An Awesome Sunset,' and the meal for tonight is in the trunk. Help me with the bags, will you, son?" Gregory said as he unbuckled his seat belt and opened the car door. After getting out of the car, he stuck his head in once more and said in his best maître d' voice, "I am sure you will all enjoy both the dinner and the show. Won't you follow me?"

That evening turned out to be one of the most fun family outings Jenny could remember. The grocery bags contained fried chicken and potato salad from the supermarket deli. There was bread from the supermarket bakery, fresh fruit from the produce department, and a bag of chocolate chip cookies for dessert. Gregory had even remembered paper plates, plastic silverware, and napkins. The Petersons always kept a blanket in the trunk, and with everyone carrying a piece of the picnic, they found a beautiful grassy spot overlooking a little lake and facing west. After the meal, there would be a beautiful sunset to finish off a beautiful day, and this family was ready to enjoy the show.

As they began to unpack the picnic, Gregory suddenly remembered something else. "Oh, I almost forgot." He reached into his jacket pocket. "There *will* be a family portrait today after all." He pulled out a disposable camera, also courtesy of the local supermarket. And with an exaggerated and heroic bow, he placed it in the middle of the blanket.

After dinner, everyone took turns taking photographs of the family. And the first passerby was stopped and coerced into taking *the* family portrait.

The Petersons—all five of them—grinning from ear to ear, standing before a lake with the sun just beginning to set in the background, looking like they did not have a care in the world. This moment in time had been forever captured with a disposable camera from the grocery store and a willing passerby. Who said that the best family portraits came from fancy studios?

Jenny gently placed the photograph back into position on the file cabinet. She truly was blessed with a wonderful family. At that moment, the phone rang, and Jenny was startled. She thought about answering it, but before she could decide if she should, there was a click. Then she heard her dad's familiar voice: "This is Professor Peterson. I can't pick up the phone at the moment. Please leave a message."

The message was from a student who wanted to make an appointment to discuss some make up work, and Jenny was glad she had not picked up the call. Glancing at the clock, she reached for her cappuccino. She took a sip and unconsciously made a face. The cappuccino had long ago gotten cold. Once again, time had slipped away.

*At this rate*, Jenny thought, *it will be dinnertime before I ever get out of here!* She grabbed her sweater, purse, and the cold cappuccino and headed for the door. Locking it behind her, Jenny headed for her car.

# INTERLUDE

Jenny settled in nicely at Montague. She enjoyed her job and the freedom that came from moving out of her parents' house. Gregory spent three days a week in Montague with her at the apartment, but the rest of the time, it was all hers. Grace had made the trip in with Gregory a few times, and she and Jenny were able to catch up on things. The visits were more frequent when Jenny first made the move, but they became farther and farther apart as time went on.

Jenny had never felt uncomfortable in Harborview with her parents after her accident, but she found out how much she appreciated time alone after the transition. It seems there comes a time in everyone's life when it is prudent to leave the nest and become a separate entity. That may take the form of a spouse and children and a family of one's own. But it could also take the form of independence and one's own space under another roof. Even Jenny's mom came to realize that Jenny needed her own space, and she could see now how the move had been good for her in spite of all of Grace's worrying.

Jenny came home to Harborview for the Thanksgiving holiday and for an occasional weekend, but she always found herself eager to return to the quiet of the Montague apartment. She kept busy with the work in the library and enjoyed the new-yet-familiar surroundings. She visited familiar places, looked up some old friends, and settled into the comfort of a new routine. Fall turned into winter, and winter brought the Christmas season. The university was closed for the winter break, and Jenny spent the holidays with her family. Richard and Beth had decided to have Christmas at their house, and Gregory, Grace, and Jenny enjoyed the change. It was the first time the family did not gather at the Peterson homestead. It was odd for Grace not to be the one preparing the meal, but she found herself enjoying a certain freedom of her own. Everyone helped out, just like in years past, but this year Beth was the woman in charge—although she found herself often deferring to Grace throughout the preparations.

The very best part of the Christmas dinner was the big announcement that came at the end of the meal. Jenny should have noticed that Richard and Beth had just picked at their food, all the while exchanging little knowing smiles. But she had been caught up in the joy of Christmas and family and had not been paying attention. Before everyone had finished eating, Richard stood up and tapped his knife on the side of his glass. "I would like to make an announcement," he said. "A toast, perhaps." He turned and gave Beth a huge grin, to which Beth responded by blushing and lifting her glass. The rest of the family looked from one to another but lifted their glasses in like manner and turned to hear what Richard had to say.

"Ahem," Richard continued. "As you know, this is the first time Beth and I have hosted Christmas dinner. We are so glad everyone is here, and we hope to be able to do this again next year." Richard paused and looked at Beth once again, who was smiling back at him. Then he looked at the family, eagerly watching him. "But next year, we are going to have to make room for one more. Maybe not up to the table yet but certainly in our lives and hearts."

At first, everyone just gave each other a quizzical look. Then Grace looked at Beth. "Beth, is it true? Are you going to have a baby?"

Beth nodded and smiled so hard that tears began to roll down her cheeks. Richard exclaimed, "I'm going to be a father!"

Everyone began talking all at once. The dinner was completely forgotten, and probably no one would have remembered the glasses they still held if Gregory had not said, "Well, then, let's drink this toast, so we can all hug the new mom-to-be. To my grandchild!"

# BEN'S Story

CHAPTER

15

*lick, whoosh, thump … Click, whoosh, thump … Click, whoosh,
thump.* The machines went on and on with seemingly endless
energy. The workers rushed to keep up with the parts as they came
down the line. The factory was hot and sticky, but there was no stopping
until the foreman blew the whistle. Despite the kerchief tied around Ben's
head, the sweat dripped into his eyes. He rhythmically wiped it away with
the back of his hand between the beats of the machine. There were no
excuses for missing a part or for not meeting an unreasonable quota. And
there was a severe price to be paid for either offense. The day began at
dawn and did not end until the sun began to set. Mercifully, the workers
were allowed an hour's siesta during the hottest part of the day—but only
if the foreman's conditions had been met satisfactorily that morning. The
workers all knew the siesta was not for their benefit but for the benefit of
the factory foreman, but no one balked at the break or asked for more.

Most of the men working in the factory had grown up in this part of
Mexico, and their fathers had done the same backbreaking work to put
food on their tables when they were growing up. This kind of work tended
to put a man into an early grave. There were not enough water breaks,
and the heat and constant movement dehydrated a person in a hurry.
Maybe some adapted better than most, but way too many others died long
before their time from heart attacks and heat strokes that could have been
prevented with more humane working conditions.

It was early summer and an especially hot day. The siesta break was a welcome bonus. Yesterday they had not been allowed one because one man had not moved quickly enough. It did not matter that he lost part of his hand in the process, and his livelihood as well. It only mattered that the machine had to be shut down and production halted while the mess was cleaned up. The workers were not allowed the privilege of sitting down. They were forced to tend to the man and clean the machine without a break, and then forced to work an extra hour in the evening to make up for the loss of time. The only man who received absolution from the mess was the one who had been given the assignment of binding the wound and taking the man home for his wife to deal with. There was no ambulance called, no doctor summoned in spite of the man's screams of agony. His own belt was used as a tourniquet, and he was half-carried home by the coworker assigned to the task.

Ben cringed at the memory of it all, even as he eased himself down to the ground under the only tree around. He was lucky enough to be one of the first men out of the factory today and rested his back against the trunk of the tree. He shut his eyes but soon opened them again and gave up his spot to an older man, who was looking very pale in spite of his weathered brown skin. Ben noticed the man was not sweating, which was a bad sign. He passed a cup of water to the man, but he refused the drink. Ben coaxed him to sip the water, and the old man closed his eyes and leaned back against the tree.

How long will this have to go on in this place? Did the foreman not realize that they could get more work out of these men with a little more humane treatment? If he continued to force the men to work in these conditions, he would soon have no one left alive to work in the factory. Ben had reasoned that a few more breaks and some fresh water during the day could go a long way toward productivity. But on the day he approached the foreman, the whole line suffered the consequences of his impudence. What was Ben doing in a place like this anyway? How did he get to this point? It was getting to be an old, sad story, one he retraced every day in his mind since he came to Mexico. And no matter the cost to himself, he was bound and determined to follow through on the commitment he made. Even if it meant dying in this crummy excuse for a job!

Benjamin Baxter had not grown up in this Mexican town, but his mother had. Her father had worked in the same factory where Ben now found himself. The day his grandfather died, Ben's mother vowed that this factory would not kill any sons she might have. Once she buried her father, Maria was determined to find a better life. She tried to convince her mother and brothers to leave, but they knew no other life. They did not have the vision of freedom that had been born in the suffering Maria. Her family forbade her to speak of leaving, but she could not bear to watch the factory suck the life from her brothers. She dreaded any future this town might hold in store for her. She had begged and begged her brothers to take the family out of this place, but they had no money and no hope. They were as resigned to this life as their late father had been. It was their fate, their destiny, and nothing could change those facts.

Maria threatened to leave on her own and cried alone in her room at night as she begged a God she did not know to help her. Maria's family gave her an ultimatum, either she straightened up and forgot this notion of leaving, or they would seek a husband for her who could control this rebellion within her. Knowing this was a very real possibility, Maria decided to bide her time and make a run for it on her own as soon as an opportunity presented itself.

The first time she tried to leave, her brothers came looking for her, found her, and dragged her back home. They locked her in her room and promised to make good on their threat to find her a husband who would teach her the discipline she should have as a woman. Maria knew her brothers loved her and that they truly thought this was the best solution for her. Maria also knew, however, that she could not endure the life she had watched her mother live.

She promised herself that her next attempt would be more successful. Fueled by desperation, Maria watched for any opportunity to flee. She kept a small bag packed and hidden, prepared to run whenever the chance came. On the outside, she tried to exemplify the repentant runaway to keep her brothers from pursuing their promise. Yet at fifteen, she knew it was only a matter of time.

Maria continued to take any opportunity to persuade her mother and brothers to leave the tyranny in which they lived under the control of the factory owner. They shushed her foolish notions that anything could change for them and urged her not to make her opinions known. They were well aware of the price of insurrection for anyone crossing the factory owner. Those bold enough to do so were dealt with in a swift and unpleasant fashion. The townspeople lived in fear, and thus, in ultimate surrender.

Growing up, Ben never knew all the details of his mother's escape. She would only share so much of the story and no more. As a child, Ben imagined many scenarios. As he grew older, each romantic escapade he had devised in his childish mind gave way to worse and unknowingly more realistic possibilities. He thought he would never know the truth. Then the day came when he was called to his mother's bedside. As she lay dying, the details he had only imagined paled in comparison to the reality she was about to reveal. And the truth he now knew would take his life in a whole new direction.

CHAPTER

# 17

Maria Baxter lay on her deathbed. The cancer had progressed quickly, and the subsequent pain and weakness had become her captor. Once again she had to surrender to a force greater than herself. It reminded her of those awful days in Mexico, when she left her family home for the last time.

The day she had longed for had finally come. Her brothers had gone on some mysterious mission for the factory owner. All Maria knew was that they were going to be gone for a few days. She did not know where he sent them or what he sent them to do. In hindsight, she was glad she never found out all the details. Whatever the job, it took them out of their small town. At the same time, Maria's mother had been called to a neighboring home to assist with the birth of the woman's baby. It seemed there were some problems developing with the delivery, and her family was beginning to panic. Maria's mother was the closest thing this miserable town had to a midwife, let alone a real doctor, so she had gone to try to help and did not know how soon she would be back home. Maria was left alone. This was the opportunity she had prayed for so desperately.

Maria tied her small bag onto her body, much as a woman might strap an infant to her bosom as she worked. She wrapped a heavy shawl around her shoulders and began to walk away. *Act natural,* she told herself as she tried not to run. Where would she go? How would she survive? Nagging fear began to grip her and threatened to turn her feet around. *I don't care if I die … as long as I don't die here,* she reminded herself. Just a few days later she would remember that thought and wish she *had* died.

Ben approached his mother's bed as quietly as he could. Maria's eyes were closed. She got so little sleep with all the pain. He couldn't tell if she were really asleep now or just attempting to rest. The doctor had ordered morphine to keep her as comfortable as possible and had assured Ben that Maria would not suffer much longer.

Maria heard the soft footsteps. She heard the quiet sound the chair made as Ben sat beside her bed. She had sent for Ben to tell him the awful truth from her past and to secure a promise from him. She wasn't sure where to begin, but she knew she did not have much more time. She slowly opened her eyes and tried to focus on her son.

"Mom." He spoke the word like it was being torn from his heart. He could hardly bear to see his mother like this. Asking how she was feeling seemed like adding fuel to an already cruel fire, so he just took her hand in his and said, "I'm here, Mom."

"Benjamin," she whispered. She closed her eyes again. Ben didn't know if she were again trying to sleep or simply did not have the strength to keep them open. He watched her pale face and noticed tears coming from her closed eyes.

"Mom, what can I do for you?" He asked in helplessness.

"I need to tell you something. I need for you to promise me …" She faltered. "I need you to promise me."

"What is it, Mom? I will do anything I can."

Maria lay still. Her eyes slowly opened again. There was a look of resolve in them that Ben had not seen in a while. He bent closer to her.

"Help me to sit up a little, Benjamin." Ben found the controls for the bed and pushed the button to raise her head. "That's good," she said.

Ben sat on the edge of the bed and once more took his mother's hand in his. "What is it, Mom?"

"I need to tell you about my past. I need to tell you how I left Mexico."

"You told me before, Mom," Ben said, wondering if the pain medication was robbing his mother of her memory. "I know you ran away from home when you were a young girl. I know that you had a rough life in Mexico. I know that you met Dad when you came to the United States."

"Yes," she said, "but there is more that you don't know. Not even your father knew."

Ben's father had died several years ago. It had devastated Maria. Ben was still a young man but had dutifully taken over as the man of the house. He still felt very protective of his sweet mother and felt the strain of the present conversation taking its toll on her. He wanted to protect her even now.

"It's OK, Mom. You don't have to tell me anything."

"No! You must listen. You must know." Maria seemed to gain a little strength with her resolve to get the story out. She took a deep breath. "Things were really bad in Mexico. There was no future there. I didn't want any son of mine to end up in that factory. I had to get away."

"I know, Mom," Ben tried to reassure her.

"I tried to convince my family to leave. I tried to tell them." Maria began to sob again.

"Just rest, Mom," Ben did not know how to comfort her.

"I prayed and prayed. Then one day everyone was gone. I had my bag packed and ready. I knew I had to go. I was afraid to get caught again, but I was more afraid of ending up like my mother." Her tone softened, and the look on her face told Ben that she was back in Mexico, reliving that day. Was that a look of regret he saw?

"I walked and walked. A truck came along, and I hid in the bushes. It went past me, and when I thought it was far enough away, I got back on the road. Then I heard it stop and turn around. I began to run. I couldn't help it. I ran as fast as I could, but it wasn't fast enough."

"You hadn't told me that part, Mom," Ben acknowledged softly. He knew the rest of the story was going to be hard to hear. But he also knew his mother would never rest until she finished. "What happened then?"

"The men stopped the truck and got out and chased me. They knocked me to the ground. They said ugly things to me, and I thought they were going to hurt me." Maria paused for a moment. "I was only fifteen," she whispered.

Ben braced himself for the words he did not want to hear. "Did they hurt you?" he asked as calmly as he could manage.

"I thought they were going to, but then another truck came along. It was the factory owner. He was such a mean man ..." Her voice drifted off in a sorrowful remembrance. Ben thought she would give in to the pain medicine this time and go to sleep. He begged the medicine to do what it was meant to do. He did not want to hear the rest of her story. He did not think he could bear it.

After a few more seconds, Maria began again with new resolve. She cleared her throat. Ben knew the sobs clogging it were just waiting to explode but his brave little mother swallowed them back.

"Señor Gonzales," she spat the name, "came over to the men. I was on the ground. He kicked me to roll me over on my back. He saw the bag strapped to me. He yanked it off, and my clothes spilled on to the ground. He looked at me and recognized me. I was so frightened. I knew how mean he could be."

"Stop, Mom. I don't want to hear anymore."

"You must," she said softly. She looked him hard in the eye. "You need to understand."

CHAPTER

# 18

Remembering that day in his mother's bedroom tortured Ben even after all these years. She had died a few days afterwards, and the only comfort Ben could find in her death was the look of relief on her face as Ben made his promise to her.

It was all over. The years of keeping those secrets to herself, Ben was sure, were far worse than the agony of her final months of the cancer. But in the end, she had revealed them all. They were all out in the open, and with the promise she secured from Ben, he was sure she was finally at peace in her last few days.

Maria's suffering had only begun to play out when her father died, and she learned to hate the factory and the town in which she was trapped. Being brought home by her brothers and locked up in her room the first time she ran away was nothing compared to the nightmare of the next time. Even now, Ben could feel the anger seething inside him as he recalled her story.

The factory owner had recognized her that day for sure. He knew she was the sister of the men he had sent away on a job, which was merely a ruse that would lead to their untimely deaths. It seems they had actually been giving Maria's suggestions some thought after all. One night after a bit too much tequila, one of her brothers had boasted about getting out of that town for good and had made a few too many comments about Señor Gonzales. But the factory owner, having ears all over town, quickly heard of their arrogance. The next day they were sent on that so-called job. The brothers felt honored to be chosen to go, but when they never returned, the townspeople knew the factory owner had gotten his point across. Fear reigned supreme again.

Of course, Maria did not learn the fate of her brothers right away. She did not have a chance to think about them or her mother over the next few hours, while Señor Gonzales had his way with her over and over and over. The next morning, Maria found herself locked in a new bedroom. She was bloodied and battered. Her clothes were torn and scattered around the room. She could barely see out of one eye; the other was completely swollen shut. She couldn't remember when she finally passed out the night before, but now, she wished she had not awakened at all.

Time stood still for her in this new nightmare. Agony was in each movement. Dying could not have been worse than this. She did not know how much time passed before someone came into the room. An older woman, about her mother's age, finally came in with some broth and some antiseptic. She made no comments or excuses for Maria's condition but tenderly cleansed and tended to her wounds. She gave Maria a cotton nightdress and coaxed her to sip some broth. Maria guessed the woman may have experienced some of Señor Gonzales's hospitality for herself. Then as quickly as she came, the woman was gone again, leaving Maria alone with her thoughts and her pain.

The room had no windows, so it was hard for Maria to judge whether it was day or night. Hours seemed like days. Maria had no idea how long she had actually been there, but all too soon, she had another visit from Señor Gonzales.

The factory owner had a whip in his hand as he came over to Maria. She cowered on the bed. He carried a lantern in the other hand. It was the first light she had seen since the woman came in to dress her wounds. Had it been hours or days? Perhaps it was all a bad dream and she would wake up soon and be back at home.

But it was not a dream. It was revenge. Señor Gonzales did not take kindly to insubordination, and that was how he interpreted her brothers' actions. It was like a drug-induced high to him to be able to exact his revenge even further on their little sister, and her mother was next in line. It gave him great pleasure to tell Maria of her brothers' demise and of his plans for her mother. No one from their family would escape his wrath. Maria begged him to leave her mother out of it. She had suffered enough and was now all alone. Maria promised him she would do anything he wanted if he would not harm her mother. And so her nightmare continued.

The factory owner finally agreed to her pleas in return for her promise that she would willingly stay and give herself to him whenever he wanted. Maria knew that even if she did not agree, he would take her whenever he wanted to anyway—by force if necessary. She did not really trust him to keep his promise, but she also knew that not making the promise was certain doom for her mother.

And so Maria played her part in the nightmare. It did not take long before Maria discovered she was pregnant. The thought of his seed inside her made her nauseated. She vowed she would *not* have his baby. She refused to tell him in hopes that his not-too-gentle visits to her would cause her to miscarry. But this baby was strong, and soon she could no longer hide the fact of her pregnancy from him. He was angry and beat her, but still the pregnancy continued. He stopped coming to her after that.

A few months later, her baby was born in the same bedroom in which she had been conceived. The woman who had nursed her wounds and given her the cotton nightdress the first night she was held captive acted as a midwife. Maria had a daughter. She wondered if her daughter would ever be allowed outside the room where Maria had spent the last year of her life. As her daughter nursed at her breast, Maria fell in love with her despite her resolve not to do so. Two days later, Maria's world was shattered again.

CHAPTER

# 19

Ben stood and put his fist into the tree. What was he doing here? All he wanted to do was to put that fist into Señor Gonzales's face. How could he have agreed to this? Was he out of his mind? What was he doing trusting a man like that?

*Oh, Jenny,* Ben thought deep in his soul. *What would you say if you only knew?*

Ben thought a lot about Jenny lately. Would she have been proud of him for upholding his end of the bargain he made with the devil? He wished she were here now to help him persevere. He didn't know if he could make it another month. And what if he did? Would that piece of dirt uphold his end of the bargain? And what if he did keep his word? What then? What would he do next?

Things had not always been like they were now. There were much happier times, and thoughts of those happier days were all Ben had now to keep him going. That and his faith. Sometimes Ben wondered how he ever existed before meeting the Savior. If only he could have told Jenny before he lost her. How excited and happy she would have been. Thoughts of his salvation were often bittersweet as they always somehow mingled with his memories of Jenny. He could not believe he had lost the one person to whom he had given his heart. He had fallen in love with her hard and doubted whether he could ever find a love like that again. How he longed to share the Savior with her.

Jenny had always been so strong in her faith. She often told Ben how much Jesus loved him. He could picture her now, tears running down her face as she tried to convince him of the Savior's love. And he had just as often scoffed at her God, who was supposed to love everyone but then let bad things happen to the people He supposedly loved so much. It had been his constant argument to all her attempts at persuasion. Jenny would smile with empathy in her eyes and tell him that someday he would understand. He understood now and longed to tell her so.

Jenny once told him she would never stop praying that the Holy Spirit would open his eyes to the truth. Her prayers had been answered. Jesus had indeed drawn Ben to Himself. And Ben longed to tell her so. Every time he relived the day he accepted Christ as his Savior, he thought of Jenny and the last time he saw her.

Ben couldn't forget the night he told Jenny that he had to go away. It was a winter's night, just after Christmas. They were sitting in the park, out in the snow, on their favorite bench facing the gazebo. The park was not far from the college where Jenny was still working after she graduated. It was winter break, so the college was closed. Jenny had spent Christmas with her family in Harborview and was back at her apartment before she left to spend New Year's with her brother, Richard, and his wife, Beth. It was getting dark, and it was snowing that delicate, soft Christmas snow that twinkled as it fell. He had put off telling her about leaving until the night before he had to leave for El Paso. He did not want to leave this heavenly creature beside him, but she had made it clear that no matter how much she cared for him, her commitment as a Christian would not allow them to marry as long as he was not a believer. He could not bear staying, and he could not bear to leave. But he had worked it out over and over in his mind until he came to the conclusion that leaving for a while would be the best thing all the way around. Besides, he had made a promise his mother, and he was determined to fulfill that promise. He had come to the city to look for information about the sister he had never known. And now that pursuit was leading him back to the very life from which his mom escaped so many years ago.

Jenny knew that Ben was on a mission to find his sister. It was what brought Jenny and Ben together in the first place. And now it seemed that the trail was leading back to where it had all begun. Ben had promised his mom that he would find and save his sister. Perhaps if Ben's mom had told him earlier, she may have had the opportunity to know her daughter. But pride and fear had kept Maria from confiding in Ben or her husband all those years. But a promise to a dying woman was something Ben could not break, even for love. Especially now that Jenny had made it clear to him they could not pursue any more of a relationship than the one they now shared. Still, it was difficult to find a way to tell Jenny he had to go. Finally, on their last night together, he just whispered, "Jenny, I have to go away."

As he relived the memory, it was still as vivid as if it had happened yesterday. After he spoke the words, he wondered if he actually said them aloud. Jenny did not move or say anything. Seconds seemed like hours. But just when he was convinced that the words had not been audible after all, he heard a small sniffle and realized Jenny was crying. She had heard him. And his words had made her cry.

Had she railied at him, he could have defended himself. Had she screamed at him, he could have attempted to calm her. Had she walked away in anger, he could have dealt with it. But she had not moved. She just wept softly as they sat there on the bench with her back snuggled to his side. His arm had been around her as they sat on the bench. His hand was draped over her shoulder, and her gloved hand was in his. One minute her back was cradled against his side, and they were watching the snowfall together. Now she was softly sobbing, and Ben's heart was breaking into a million pieces.

How could he have hurt her like that? There must have been a better way. And now, how could he bear to leave? This was the woman he loved, and he had just caused her tears.

In hindsight, Ben could look back and realize how strong Jenny had really been. Perhaps her faith played a big part in how she reacted. Perhaps she was just wise beyond her years. She knew when he said those words that what he told her must come to pass. She knew she could not stop him from fulfilling the destiny he had taken up on himself to fulfill. And she knew she had no hold on him as long as he remained an unbeliever in the Savior to Whom she had committed her life.

When she finally turned toward him, he took her chin in his hand and tipped her face up so he could look directly into her reddened eyes, mercifully hidden in the darkness. He could never have gone if he had seen the tearstains on her face.

Even now, he could again feel the lump that had constricted his throat and the pain that had gripped his heart when she finally spoke, "God's ways are not our ways, and His thoughts are not our thoughts." She paused. Just when he thought he could bear the silence no longer, she continued, "There is a reason this is happening now. There is a bigger plan for both of us. We were brought together for a time, and now we must be apart for a time." Ben could feel his own tears moistening his cheeks and was once again grateful for the darkness.

He couldn't understand her reaction. He was not prepared to handle this kind of response. Jenny took Ben's hands in hers and, as she stood, she drew him to his feet. They embraced and held each other for what seemed like an eternity. What he would give to be able to feel that embrace again … to even have the hope that he would feel that embrace again.

They had agreed to keep in touch. He would call her as often as he could, and she would wait for his calls. After he located his sister and kept his promise to his mother, he would come back to Jenny. They had agreed it would be too difficult to walk back to Jenny's apartment and have to say goodbye again, so they went their separate ways. Ben could scarcely stand to watch Jenny walk across the park to her apartment, but he kept his distance. He watched until he was sure she was home safely. Then he turned and walked away.

If he had only known it would be the last time he would ever see her.

C H A P T E R

## 20

The whistle blew, and Ben was jolted from his memories back to the reality he had grown to despise. Siesta was over, and the men were making their way back to the machines that defined their existence. Ben had the days numbered until he had fulfilled his promise to Señor Gonzales. Now if only his temper could stay in check, and if he could survive the next three weeks.

Ben resumed his regular position on the line. Soon the familiar cadence of the machines and the synchronized brow-wiping monopolized his time. He could usually focus on work and shut out the thoughts and memories that plagued him in his off-hours, but today, even the horrendous factory conditions could not keep his mind from working overtime.

He was back again at his mother's bedside. Her tears were uncontrollable as she came to the end of her confessions. Two days after her baby girl was born, the two men who had chased her down on the road the day she ran away from home stormed into her room. Without explanation, the baby was taken from her arms and handed to the same woman who had been her midwife and nurse. The men grabbed Maria and forced her outside. The sunlight burned, and instinct made her close her eyes. When was the last time she had seen daylight? She stumbled as they dragged her to the waiting truck. One man opened the door and shoved her inside. She landed against another person. Forcing her eyes open, she looked at the woman in the seat next to her. It was her mother. She looked very old, very sad, and very frightened. Maria threw her arms around her as the door slammed closed. The other man climbed in behind the steering wheel, and they were off.

Maria did not know what was happening. She asked the man and her mother what was going on. Her mom was too frightened to say anything, but she kept looking first at the man and then at the daughter she had thought was lost to her. Maria, however, had been through too much to be frightened now. She reached over, grabbed the steering wheel, and turned it hard. The truck went careening off the road. The man swore but managed to regain control just before the truck hit a tree. Once back in control, the man slowed the truck, reached across Maria's mother, and slapped Maria—hard. "Don't try that again if you know what is good for you," he snarled.

"Where are you taking us? Stop this truck immediately," Maria demanded.

The man laughed an evil laugh. "I would like nothing better than to stop this truck," he said with a hiss. "I would like to stop it and kill both of you myself, but Señor Gonzales has given me strict orders. And we all know what happens if his orders are not followed exactly."

"What exactly are his orders?" Maria asked boldly.

"Well, I guess it wouldn't hurt to let you know your fate," he answered, seemingly enjoying his upper hand. "You are both going to disappear. By the way, Señor Gonzales wanted me to remind you that he kept his promise." He glared at Maria.

"What promise?" Maria's mother squeaked, finding her voice.

"Señor Gonzales promised not to kill you if your daughter agreed to be his willing little play toy." The man sneered. "But Señor Gonzales has tired of her, and now you are both going to disappear forever."

"But what about my baby?" Maria sobbed, suddenly losing a bit of her boldness.

"Oh, yeah. Señor Gonzales said that his flesh and blood does not leave his camp, even if her mother is of no more use to him."

The truck turned off the road and traveled down a trail through the woods. They had gone only a short distance when the man pulled the truck up next to a cargo van.

"End of the road, ladies," he said and spat. Maria looked for a place to run. Even if she could get away, what about her mother? At that moment the van doors opened, and two more men came over to the truck.

"Is this it?" one man asked. "Is this all we get?"

"This is it. Take them, and make sure they don't ever come back."

"Oh, they are as good as gone," he assured the other man. And with that, Maria and her mother were shoved into the back of the van, and the door slammed shut.

CHAPTER

# 21

The whistle finally blew, signaling the end of the day. The machines began to stop one at a time. Soon there was only silence. The men were all too tired to even make polite conversation as they dragged themselves to the door. It was Saturday, and tomorrow was finally a day off for the weary men. Even Señor Gonzales respected the Lord's day.

Ben made his way to the small room he rented from one of the factory workers and collapsed on his cot. His mind went to his sister. Juanita was four years older than he was. He had tracked her down only after his mother made him promise to search for her. If he found her, he had promised his mother that he would do everything he could to save her. He was not sure what he was going to save her from, but nonetheless, he had promised his mother.

After his mother died, Ben began to search for his sister. All he knew was that she had been left in the town where his mother grew up, left with a man his mother despised and who was mean enough to do almost anything imaginable and then some. Ben did not even know the name of the town, just that there was a factory there owned by a tyrant who kept the town controlled by fear. He did, however, know his mother's last name and her brothers' names for she often told happy stories of them as children. He knew that his grandmother, Consuelo, had been with his mother when they arrived in the United States. What he did not know was how exactly they had gotten from Mexico into the United States. He knew that eventually his mother fell in love with his dad and married him in the United States. Now if he could just connect all the dots.

So Ben went to Montague. It was the closest city with a library big enough to house the resources he needed to begin a search. The city library suggested he try the library at the university. They offered classes in family ancestry and had a large section of their library devoted to genealogy. The day he went to Montague University Library was the day he met the most beautiful girl he had ever seen. She had auburn curls and green eyes that he could get lost in every time she smiled. Her name was Jenny.

CHAPTER

## 22

Jenny and Ben searched and searched but could find no information on either his mother or her family. It seemed like the town she came from was nonexistent, and whatever factory there was in that town merely a myth. But the time they had worked together had not been a waste by any means. Jenny and Ben developed a friendship that blossomed into an even more meaningful relationship. Looking back on their time together, Ben could only wish it had lasted much longer.

When the Mexico search yielded no results, and they were at the point of giving up altogether, Jenny suggested they try to trace Ben's father's family. Perhaps they would find something else that would link the two families besides a marriage certificate. They learned that Ben's father had been born in El Paso. He was an only child, but his father had an uncle who still lived there. It wasn't much, but it was the only lead Ben had. When everything else they knew to do had been exhausted, Ben decided to make the trip to Texas. He contacted his great-uncle, who graciously invited him to come and visit. So with a plan in motion, he said goodbye to Jenny in the park and left the next morning to begin his quest.

Driving to Texas had taken him a few days, and he spent the time alone in his car in tortured thought. Each mile he put between him and Jenny screamed out for him to turn around. The rhythmic sound of tires on asphalt seemed to say, "Go back, go back, go back." Each break he took and each rest area he visited tempted him to turn around, but they were nothing compared to the nights in shabby motels on the way. It was all he could do to keep heading south after each stop. By his last day, he had finally convinced himself to stick to the plan. He decided it was best to just buckle down to the task at hand, see what he could find out, do his best to keep his promise to his mother, get it all behind him, and then go back to Jenny. And with his new resolve, Ben at last found himself pulling into the driveway at his great-uncle Lewis's home.

CHAPTER

## 23

The alarm sounded, and Ben willed himself to wake up. He was so exhausted from the week at the factory that he could easily have slept through until Monday morning. But this was his weekend to go back to Texas, and the quick nap was only so he could make the trip without falling asleep at the wheel. He made it a point to make regular trips back to his great-uncle's house. Partly so he could look like he was just a frequent visitor across the border, but even more so that he could go to church and be revived. The people at his great-uncle's church had accepted Ben as family right away. They witnessed his transformation as he became a child of God. They were present in the church the night Ben surrendered to the Savior and accepted the salvation He offered. They watched Ben grow in his faith, and they prayed for him to be able to fulfill the promise he made to his mother. Even after all these months, on some of his worst days, when he just wanted to walk away from his whole situation, Ben could feel the prayers of those faithful saints at Faith Community Church. "Thank You, Father, for their faithfulness," Ben whispered as he pulled himself up from the small cot and headed for the door.

It did not take long to get to the border and cross into Texas. He had made the trip so many times now that the process had become rote, and the agents there were like old friends. When he originally began his trips into Mexico, Ben claimed that he was doing research as the reason for his visits. They had quit asking him, and he left it at that. It was the truth at the time. In the beginning he made frequent day trips across the border, visiting every cantina he could find in the hopes that someone would know of a small town with a factory run by a man named Gonzales. At first, the locals were hesitant to talk to a stranger, but Ben eventually began to fit in. Raised in a bilingual home had its advantages, and his heritage made his appearance more Mexican than gringo. Besides, with enough tequila, most people didn't notice the difference in his accent anyway.

It had taken about a month, but Ben eventually heard about Señor Gonzales and his factory town. Over the next few weeks, he gleaned every detail he could without appearing too interested. From what he had learned in the cantinas and remembered from his mother's horror stories, Ben did not want to become a person of interest on Gonzales's radar. It seemed he had been successful because when he finally made an appearance at the factory in the guise of looking for work, no one acted suspicious, and there were no immediate repercussions to his actions. It appeared that Ben had indeed slipped in under the radar.

Ben had chosen to take on the façade of a drifter. Even though he drove a beat-up old car, his story was that he was just passing through and had run out of money. He asked for some temporary work to earn enough money to move on. Quotas were high at the factory, and since the foreman had just lost a couple more men, he signed Ben on without even consulting the boss. Ben had not seemed like a threat of any kind, and they could use his youth and strength on the line. And so Ben became another workhorse for an evil master.

The "town," Ben discovered, wasn't a legitimate town at all. It was more of a compound. It reminded Ben of what an old Southern plantation might have been like. The master's grand house and necessary outbuildings were magnificent, while the slaves lived in shanties surrounding the fields. The factory was akin to the fields, and the workers were more like the slaves of old than modern employees. There were no government regulations or guaranteed paychecks. Meager pay was always in cash and always subject to the master's whims. The compound also boasted a small cantina and a mercantile, which was the only source of groceries and supplies for the townsfolk. And as was the case in Appalachian coal mining towns of old, most of the factory workers "owed their souls to the company store."

For the first few days on the job, Ben slept in his car. But he soon found a coworker in need of extra cash with a cot for rent. That was all Ben needed for the short time he planned to be there. And a worker bitterly in hock to the boss might turn out to be a valuable source of information. A year later, the cot was still Ben's home, and he had all the information he cared to know.

CHAPTER

## 24

It was getting late when Ben pulled into Uncle Lewis's driveway. The porch light was a welcome sight for this soul-weary man. Uncle Lewis would be expecting him and would still be up to greet him. But first he had to get past Mac. Before Ben had the chance to turn off the ignition, Mac was at the driver's side door. He was an old dog, but he could still get off the porch and to Ben's car in record time. Ben opened the door, and the German shepherd backed up only far enough to allow Ben to get out of the car before stepping forward again to nuzzle Ben's hand in a canine welcome. Ben knelt on one knee and gave the dog a huge hug and a quick scratch before they both made their way to the porch and into the house.

"Hello, there," Uncle Lewis called. "Coffee is still hot and relatively fresh if you're interested."

Ben detoured through the kitchen, pouring himself a cup of coffee on his way to join his great-uncle in the living room. Melting into an overstuffed La-Z-Boy, Ben released a grateful sigh. "Mmmmm, just what I needed," Ben said, sipping the dark hot liquid. It didn't matter that at this time of night the coffee was decaf. It was a welcome change from the swill he still had not gotten used to in Mexico.

"Tough week?" Uncle Lewis asked rhetorically. He didn't need an answer to that one. Just looking at Ben told him more than he needed to know. In a year's time, Ben seemed to have aged ten years.

"Let's just say I am looking forward to a hot shower and a real bed."

The refreshing air-conditioning, comfy chair, and soothing drink were rapidly doing their magic on Ben, and he could barely keep his eyes open.

They sat in easy silence for a while. Then his uncle suggested, "How about we just catch up in the morning, then? It's past my bedtime, and I can see you aren't going to be much good for conversation tonight." Reaching down to give the dog's ear a scratch, he said to his constant companion, "Come on, Mac. Let's go to bed." Both man and dog made their way to the stairs and slowly began their climb.

Ben watched them go and downed the last of his coffee. He knew if he did not follow suit, his uncle would find him still sleeping in the same chair come morning. With great effort, Ben pulled himself up, turned off the lights, and headed to his own bed. The shower would have to wait until morning.

CHAPTER

25

Morning came way too soon, and Ben moaned as he rolled over. Sunlight streamed in the window. There was a smell of bacon in the air, and Ben's stomach growled in automatic response. As Ben slowly became fully awake, he remembered he had not bothered to eat the night before. Rested and renewed from a good night's sleep, Ben got up and headed for the shower.

Standing in the shower, Ben let the warm water wash over him. His uncle's humble home was like the fanciest hotel in the world compared to the facilities he had to put up with in Mexico. He thought of his sister, who had never known any other way of life. What would she think of the world outside her miserable existence? Did she even know she was miserable? Were his efforts all for naught? Did she even want to be rescued? As the time got closer and closer to her promised release, Ben was plagued by those thoughts more and more. Would Gonzales keep his word? "Dear Lord, please let it be so," Ben prayed.

The water had gotten cold when Ben finally and reluctantly turned off the refreshing flow. Once out of the shower, the smell of sizzling bacon and fresh coffee restimulated his stomach's automatic response. Ben picked up his pace and hurriedly dressed. In a few minutes, he was anxiously sitting down to the biggest breakfast he had seen since his last trip home. As hungry as we was, he knew his uncle would pray before they ate. He suddenly realized how much he actually longed to hear the faithful Christian lift his voice to their mutual Savior.

"Good morning, Lord. Thank you so much for seeing us through the night. Thank You for seeing Ben home safely. Thank You for never leaving us or forsaking us. You are so very faithful." His uncle's pause was palpable as both Ben and Lewis took in the awesomeness of God's promises. "We know that Your plans come about in Your timing, but sometimes, the wait is so hard for us. Help Ben to stay the course that You have led him on. Protect him, guide him, strengthen him, be his ever-present help in times of need. Watch over Juanita. Bless this food to our bodies. May we always be quick to give You praise. In Jesus's name, Amen."

The food was almost as good as the Christian communion the men shared. As Ben smeared jelly on yet another biscuit and took a huge bite, Lewis said, "So catch me up. What's been going on since we last talked?"

Ben had to swallow before he could respond. "The same old stuff, I guess." He took another bite of eggs, and while he was still chewing them, popped a piece of crisp bacon into his mouth.

In a more serious tone, Lewis asked, "How are you holding up, son?"

Ben hesitated for a moment, put his fork down, wiped the jelly from mouth, and confessed to his uncle in a serious tone of his own, "I don't know if I can last three more weeks." Ben paused. In his wisdom, Lewis let the silence fill the room. Ben continued, "What if it isn't worth it? What if that monster doesn't keep his bargain?" The words tore from somewhere deep in Ben's soul, betraying his fears.

"When Jacob fell in love with Rachel, he agreed to work seven long years for her. When the time came for Rachel's father to send Rachel to Jacob, he sent her older sister, Leah, instead. It was a cruel trick, but Jacob was determined and agreed to work another seven years for Rachel. In the end, God was faithful and gave Jacob the desires of his heart." Lewis related once again the story Ben had become familiar with shortly after he bargained with Gonzales. Ben had agreed to work in his factory for a year, and Gonzales had promised that he would let Juanita leave with Ben when the year was up.

Pedro Gonzales had never been a father to Juanita. Although she knew he was her father, the only parent Juanita had ever known was Mama Bella. Isabella was the woman who raised Juanita, but both of them were his mere servants. He had never wanted Juanita as his daughter. He just did not want anyone else to have her, especially not her birth mother. He had his fill of Maria when she became pregnant with Juanita, but her death would have been too easy. Besides, at the time, Gonzales had not finished exacting his revenge on her family for daring to even think of leaving town. So he decided that if leaving was what they really wanted, he would arrange for her to leave, and he would be sure the only remaining family member left with her. Maria would be devastated without her baby, and Consuelo would suffer with her. Not only would it serve his purpose, but it would send a message to everyone else as well. So right after Juanita was born, Gonzales had his men grab Maria's mother and take her and Maria away for good. Everyone in town heard of it, and a new fear enhanced the submission Gonzales already had from them. And at the same time, it fueled his egotistical desire for even more power.

"I know the story, Uncle," Ben said sadly. "I know God is faithful. But what if this bargain wasn't what God had in mind? What if rescuing my sister is only a promise I made to Mom and not what God wants for Juanita? What if Gonzales doesn't keep his end of the bargain? Juanita is too afraid to leave without his permission. It was all I could do to convince her to agree to it once I made the bargain with Gonzales."

"As far as I see it, Gonzales has two choices, Ben. He can either renege on his bargain or keep his word. I think he has probably made a name for himself by keeping his word, and I don't mean in a good way. None of his threats are idle threats. He is known for doing what he says he will do. If he reneges on the promise he made to you, he will send a message to the people that perhaps he will not follow through on his threats either. He will never take that risk. His promises, no matter how good or evil, keep the people in line."

Although Lewis's argument made sense to Ben, it did not relieve all the anxiety Ben felt. Still, it gave him food for thought. And if Gonzales did decide to renege, perhaps Ben could somehow use that same psychology on the man himself. That thought alone brought an ever-so-tiny smile to Ben's face.

"It's getting late," Lewis pointed out. "Eat up, or we'll be late for church."

CHAPTER

## 26

Ben and Lewis arrived at church in plenty of time. Before they could get to their seats, however, Ben was surrounded by church members. Somehow Lewis managed to slip past the mob and settled into his regular spot. The church was small enough to be like one big, happy family, so when someone missed a Sunday, the others noticed, and the missing member got the royal welcome on his or her return. Ben only managed to attend every few Sundays, so this was a common reception for him—like the father welcoming home the prodigal son over and over. The love he felt at this church went a long way in sustaining him through the time away from them. *I should probably tell them that*, he thought as he finally made his way to his seat.

Ben had not always felt that way. He had been skeptical the first time he attended Faith Community. He had only gone out of respect for his great-uncle's hospitality. His great-aunt Hattie had died a few years before Ben came to Texas, and his uncle lived alone. Ben could tell right away upon meeting his uncle for the first time that Lewis was a man of faith. He had reminded Ben a little of Jenny. So when Lewis invited him to go to church, he felt compelled to accept the invitation.

Ben had sat stiffly in the pew with his uncle that first Sunday. Everyone had gone out of their way to make him feel welcome, but Ben felt he had nothing in common with any of them. They all believed wholeheartedly in a loving God. But Ben couldn't get past the same argument he used when Jenny tried to share her faith with him. How could a God who was so loving let His children experience what his mother had gone through? And to top it all off, he had just found out a few days before that his precious Jenny had been taken from him too. Where was God when she needed Him? It was all too much to bear, and at that time, he had no use for God. He tried to back out of going to the church, but his uncle was insistent, and Ben was too grieved to fight him. He went out of obligation, having already decided he would never go back again.

Funny how things had changed. Ben mused on his journey to Christ as he listened to the music all around him. In hindsight, he was certain that Jenny's prayers had played a huge part in his coming to faith. She had promised to pray for him. Ben had not understood before, but he did now. If only she had lived to see the fruit of those prayers. How proud she would have been of him.

Ben stood with the rest of the congregation as they worshipped. But his mind was not on the hymn but on that fateful day when he learned of Jenny's accident. It was a Thursday. He could remember it as if it were only moments ago. On arriving in Texas, Ben had tried to call Jenny to let her know he had made the trip safely. He left a message on her answering machine. Over the week that followed, Ben made numerous calls to Jenny's apartment and left as many messages—until the day the answering machine announced that her mailbox was full. At first he thought Jenny had prolonged her New Year's visit with her brother. But after the following weekend, Ben was sure Jenny would have returned to work at the university library. Ben thought maybe she didn't want to talk to him, but he couldn't reconcile in his mind the fact that her answering machine was still full. Even if she were avoiding his calls, surely she would have cleared the messages.

Then came the day he got the message that her number had been disconnected. Something was wrong. Finally, in desperation, he called the college. The receptionist in the library confirmed that Jenny had not been back to work since the school reopened after winter break. The woman was hesitant about giving out any information, but when Ben pushed her, she finally told him about the accident. Ben was desperate for details, but the woman would not give him any more information. Ben begged. Finally, the woman suggested that Ben try calling Jenny's parents. Ben didn't have their number but remembered that Jenny's father was a professor at the college. He asked to be transferred to his office.

The transfer only took a few seconds, but it seemed like an eternity. Why did he leave her? Why? Why? Why?

"Professors' offices," a woman's voice answered. "How may I direct your call?"

"Professor Peterson, please."

"One moment," the woman said. *Click, ringggg ... ringgg ... ringgg ...* "Hello, Greg Peterson."

"Professor Peterson," Ben began, "this is Ben Baxter. I am a friend of Jenny's."

Gregory Peterson immediately knew who was on the phone, and he knew why Ben was calling. This was the friend Jenny had introduced to him and Grace over dinner at the apartment in Montague last year. He also remembered what that meeting had done to his wife. In her present state, Jenny wouldn't remember Ben anyway. In a split-second, Gregory made a decision he often revisited, wondering if he should have handled the call differently.

"Yes, Ben, I remember you," Gregory replied stoically. "Are you calling about Jenny?"

"Yes, sir. I just found out about her accident. Is she OK?" Ben held his breath.

There was a pause. "No, Ben. I'm sorry. She was in Bluffton Hospital. She had a head injury and lapsed into a coma." Gregory stopped there, leaving the rest of the story to play out in Ben's mind. He didn't actually lie to Ben. He just chose to leave out a few facts. Unless pressed for more details, Gregory would leave it at that. Ben reacted exactly as Gregory had hoped.

Ben felt like he had been shot! Grief overwhelmed him. He couldn't speak. He couldn't think. His knees weak, he slumped to the floor. At some point, Professor Peterson must have thought the conversation was over because it was only when he heard the dial tone that Ben was pulled back into reality.

Ben felt like his world had ended. First, he lost his father when he was only a young teen. Then he watched the mother he adored suffer with cancer, which had seemed unbearable, until the confession she made and the promise she begged for made the cancer seem like the least of her sufferings. His precious mother had been taken from him, and now the woman he loved was gone. What did he have to live for now?

At that moment, the bitterness gave way to determination. Ben put up a shell around his heart that he thought no one could penetrate. He decided he would not be hurt again. He would never again let anyone in. But he did not realize how persistent and patient Jesus could be.

The congregation sat down again, and Ben almost missed it. He was still standing when his uncle gently tugged on Ben's shirt, bringing him back to the present. As he sat down, he decided he better try to concentrate on the service for the rest of the hour.

The pastor made some announcements, they sang a few more hymns, and then it was time for the message. Ben settled in, determined to concentrate on the Word of God upon which the pastor would expound. He needed his batteries recharged. He needed his faith to be lifted. Three more weeks. Could he survive? Not without the strength that only God could give.

Pastor Mike began, "Our scripture for today comes from the letter of Paul to the Philippians. Turn with me to Philippians chapter 4 and verses 4-7." Ben turned easily to the passage and began to read along as Pastor Mike read, "Rejoice in the Lord always. Again I will say, rejoice! Let your gentleness be known to all men. The Lord is at hand. Be anxious for nothing, but in everything by prayer and supplication, with thanksgiving, let your requests be made known to God; and the peace of God, which surpasses all understanding, will guard your hearts and minds through Christ Jesus."

Pastor Mike paused a moment before beginning the sermon, but he didn't need to say another word. The Lord had already spoken peace into Ben's heart. The next three weeks might be difficult, but with God's help, Ben would make it through. His eyes were drawn to a verse a little farther down on the page, one which he had previously highlighted in his Bible, verse 13: "I can do all things through Christ who strengthens me."

C H A P T E R

## 27

The message served to renew Ben's faith. The fellowship served to renew his hope. The prayers of the saints served to renew his determination. As Ben tried to make his way out of the little sanctuary, church members pressed in around him until he felt surrounded by not only his own trust in the Savior but wrapped in the trust the others had. It was like they had wrapped him in a blanket of faith. Promises of prayer and words of encouragement reached not only his ears but also his heart as he finally made his way out to Uncle Lewis's truck.

The trip back to the house was quick. Uncle Lewis set out the fixings for sandwiches and once again offered a prayer of thanksgiving for the food. Ben made his sandwich and carried it into the living room, where he once again melted into the overstuffed La-Z-Boy. He wanted to take advantage of the comfort for just a little while longer, before he had to set out for Mexico once again.

"I probably will not make it back here again before the next three weeks are done," Ben thought out loud. "Hopefully I will have my sister in tow when I come back for good."

Uncle Lewis chewed contemplatively. He was not sure Ben was looking for a response. After a few minutes he asked, "Do you have plans for getting her across the border? And what are your plans for her once you have her here?"

With all the plans Ben had made, all the time he had spent convincing Juanita to come with him, and all the prayers he had prayed for God to make it all come to pass, somehow he had not thought of those particulars. He could feel something akin to panic begin to rise within him. How could he have neglected to make a plan? What was he thinking? What would he do if they would not let her cross the border?

"I don't know," Ben replied. But Ben's answer was not that simple. It was not just a statement.

Uncle Lewis watched the color drain from his face and could hear the panic growing in his voice. The remnants of the sandwich Ben had been devouring just moments ago lay uneaten on the plate. Ben looked at his uncle with such confusion and perplexity that Lewis felt compelled to speak. "Did your mother tell you how she came into the United States?"

"No. At least I don't recall her sharing that part of her experience. Her story sort of ended with her being thrown into the cargo van with her mother. The next part I remember was a happier time, when she met Dad. I guess she left a lot out. I thought I had the whole story. It was so very difficult for her to tell me what she did. She was so weak and in so much pain that I didn't press her for any more details."

"Well, I may be able to help you with a few details, but only if you finish your sandwich," his uncle said, trying to lift the mood in the room. He knew that if Ben did not know the rest of the story it would be hard for him to hear some of it.

Ben offered his uncle a forced smile but complied with his request. The sandwich did not taste as good as it had a short while ago. The bread tasted sandy, and the ham went down hard when he tried to swallow. The lump in his throat was nearly preventing easy passage, but he compelled the food to make its way into his stomach. Each step of the normal, daily routine became an act of the will instead of unconscious habit. Once completed, he turned his attention to his uncle.

Lewis cleared his throat and began. "Your great-aunt Hattie, my wife, was still very much alive back then. She worked at the immigration center and played a huge role in your mother's story. But I also think that God was even more instrumental in the timing of the events."

Ben began to relax a bit. *So far, so good*, he thought.

"I was not really privy to all of the details, mind you, only those Hattie could share with me. Evidently there was a sting operation going on at the time. Agents had been watching a sex-trafficking ring bringing girls into the United States from Mexico. I don't know any of the details as to how they were getting the girls across the border, just that they were watching for an opportunity to intercept them. That's how your mother and grandmother were discovered in the back of a van."

Ben gasped. Had his mother known about that? Was she slated for the sex trade? Surely his grandmother would not have been a candidate. Would she have been eliminated? As he thought about the ramifications, he began to understand why his uncle believed God played a part in the timing of events. Why the raid on that van on that day? What happened to the men who were to deliver his mother and grandmother to their fates? The more he thought, the less he heard his uncle, until Ben realized Uncle Lewis had stopped to let Ben take it all in.

"I hope Mom did not know about that part of her experience."

"I don't think she did. Or if she did, I think the rescue overshadowed the what-ifs."

"Thanks," Ben said. "That is comforting. What happened next?"

Lewis cleared his throat again and continued. "Your mother and grandmother were taken to the immigration center. I believe they were questioned and had medical attention, but they were not held long. That's where your aunt Hattie comes in." Ben couldn't help but notice the smile on his uncle's face when he talked about his late wife. How he must have loved her.

"Well, like I said, I don't know all the details or how the system works, but Hattie was assigned to their case. Somehow, they were granted asylum due to the extreme circumstances. Something about because sending them back would be life-threatening."

Lewis took a big drink of iced tea. Ben tried to digest the information he had just been given. He was still confused as to how they got out of the immigration center and where they went from there. Ben waited for "the rest of the story," as Paul Harvey used to say.

"And ..." he prompted.

"Oh, yeah. Well it seems that your mom and grandmother needed a sponsor, someone who would take them in, provide a place for them to live, help them find jobs. You know, those kinds of things."

"OK," Ben responded, trying to coerce the rest of the story from his uncle.

"Well, Hattie took a liking to both of them and agreed to be their sponsor. That's how they ended up at our house."

"What?" Ben asked in astonishment. "They lived here?"

"Well, only for a little while. But it was here that Maria met your father. He was my great-nephew, you know. He and his parents were here for some sort of family thing. Maybe it was Memorial Day or a family reunion. Nope, it was definitely Memorial Day because it was the beginning of summer and a federal holiday, so the center was closing for the long weekend. That's probably why Hattie volunteered to sponsor them, so they wouldn't be stuck there in detention. She had a heart of gold, your aunt." Again, the smiled filled Uncle Lewis's face. "We kept them with us for a year or so. They both took classes to learn English. Consuelo found a job as a housekeeper and did well. She worked for nice people. Eventually she and your mom got a small apartment, but they visited often. So did your dad. He spent summers with us sometimes. They fell in love early, and the rest is history."

Ben sat back. *Ah, finally the happy memories*, he thought. He basked in the love complete strangers lavished upon his mother and grandmother. He never knew that part of the story. He was so glad he had tracked down his great-uncle while trying to locate his sister. How would he have made it this far without him?

His sister! Yes, that's what began this trip down memory lane. Just what was he going to do about his sister?

CHAPTER

# 28

"So Uncle," Ben began, "just how are we going to bring Juanita home?"

"I don't know, son." Uncle Lewis hung his head, and his elderly shoulders drooped. "I wish your aunt was here. She would have some ideas for sure."

They sat in silence for quite a while. Ben looked at the clock and realized he had better start back to Mexico. He had three weeks to go to fulfill his agreement with Señor Gonzalez. He couldn't worry now that the man might renege. Ben had to trust God. Only God could make the way straight. Only God could work in his sister's heart and make her want to come with him. Only God could cause, "all things to work together for good." This was his only and very best hope. He sighed deeply.

As Ben eased himself out of the recliner and began saying his goodbyes to his uncle, the elderly man looked deep in thought.

"What is it, Uncle?"

"Well, I don't know if it is anything at all, but do you remember meeting Phoebe Collins at church?"

"Phoebe Collins, Phoebe Collins." Ben tried to place her. "Is she the elderly lady who sits right up in the front row? Gray hair but very spry for her age?"

"Yes! That's her exactly. You know, she worked with Hattie way back then. She probably remembers your mother's case. And she still works at the immigration center part time. I wonder if she could help?"

"I'll take any help I can get," Ben replied enthusiastically. "Can we call her before I set out?"

"Can't hurt to try. I'll look up her number," Uncle Lewis said over his shoulder. He was already on a mission to locate the church directory.

CHAPTER

## 29

Phoebe had been a huge help. She did remember Maria and Consuelo. She remembered Hattie working on their case, and she remembered how much she admired Hattie for all her efforts to make their transition to the United States easy, legal, and quick. Once she connected the story to Ben's quest, she was more than willing to offer her suggestions.

As Ben had traveled back to Mexico after that conversation, he could not help but praise God for His faithfulness. His story was about to come full circle. The pieces were all falling into place. How Jenny would have rejoiced with him as he praised the God who was such a big part of her life for being just as big in his life right now.

Jenny. Oh, Jenny. His perfect Jenny. How much he still loved her. Once this quest was over, how would he go on? Ben resolved that he would throw himself entirely into his sister's life. He would spend so much effort on Juanita that he would be able to block Jenny from his thoughts. *Why, Lord, did You need to take her?*

The border was just ahead. He crossed easily without incident. *Only one more crossing*, he thought, *and my sister will be with me. And this will be almost over.* He began his countdown clock. Twenty-one days and counting.

CHAPTER

# 30

After work on Monday, Ben went to the cantina to talk to Juanita. He needed reassurance that all his efforts had not been in vain. She was busy serving customers. He saw no one he knew. The men he worked with could not afford to come and drink tequila. Even if they could afford it, they were too exhausted by the end of the day. These customers must be Gonzalez's men. That thought had not occurred to him before. He knew the boss had ears everywhere, but Ben had not factored in that every ear in the cantina was a loyal hotline directly to Gonzalez. He knew that Gonzalez had been made aware of every visit to Juanita here, but it was the only place he could see her. Ben did not know exactly where she lived with Mama Bella, but he had neither been invited nor allowed to see her there.

Eventually she came to sit with him. Juanita did not know what to make of her brother. He had told her of her mother and the promise he made to her to rescue Juanita from this life. But did she really want to leave? Sure, she would never marry here. Her father would not allow that. Even if he would, no man would dare seek her hand for fear of him. But what other kind of life was there? This was all she knew.

Juanita had been afraid to tell Mama Bella about Ben when he first approached her with the story of being her brother and coming to rescue her. Mama Bella loved her, but she, too, was afraid of Juanita's father. She had been subject to his attentions many times in her life. She knew how brutal he could be. She was still in his employ and would never cross him, not even for Juanita.

But eventually she broached the subject with Mama Bella. Ben told her that he had made a deal with her father. Ben would work for him without pay for one year if Gonzalez would agree to let Juanita go with him when that time was up. If Ben was telling her the truth, then her father already knew of his plans, so she felt talking to Mama Bella would not obligate her to go to her father.

Juanita was surprised when Mama Bella sided with Ben. She made Juanita promise not to tell her father of their conversations, and once she received the promise, she began to confirm Ben's story about how their mother came to become pregnant with Juanita. She confirmed that when she was just a newborn, Señor Gonzales sent her mother away. Mama Bella either did not know any other details or at least would not share anything else. But it was enough to make Juanita at least consider Ben's plan.

Now, almost a year later, Juanita had a lot of time to consider her options. If her father had made this agreement with Ben, then she really had no other choice than to go with him. Her father would not go back on his word and make people think he was weak. Nor would he go back on his word because of any kind of affection for his daughter. Juanita knew how much he despised her. He only kept her in the beginning to hurt her mother. She realized she would never have the chance of having a family of her own. And what would happen to her when Mama Bella died? Where would she go, and how would she support herself? She received no pay for her work at the cantina, and she didn't expect that to change in the future.

No matter how scary her immediate future might be, she had resigned herself to her new fate. It was not exactly how Ben hoped she would feel, but at least he was sure she would willingly accompany him when the time came. Three weeks was going to feel like forever.

CHAPTER

# 31

As it turned out, the days did not stretch out as Ben had anticipated. They worked him even harder at the factory, increasing his quota to a nearly impossible amount. He worked hard and long. When he reached his cot in the evenings, he fell asleep with no time to think about his remaining days, so the countdown clock moved quickly.

On the last day of Ben's agreed-upon term of service, Pedro Gonzalez put in an appearance at the factory. His foremen were extra hard on the men. The men were extra careful not to make any mistakes. Everyone knew the consequences if the boss sensed any lack of enthusiasm on their parts. There was no siesta that day.

Right before the factory was to shut down for the day, Gonzalez called Ben out. Ben was not sure what to expect. He offered up a quick, simple, and silent prayer: *Lord, God, the time has come. Hear my prayer and the prayers of all the saints who are praying especially for me today. Glorify Yourself now. Grant our requests. In Jesus's name, Amen.*

Gonzalez was loud and obnoxious. He wanted all his foremen to hear because he wanted them to tell the version of the narrative he wanted to portray. "You!" he bellowed. "I want you out of here. You are fired. Don't even go home to pack. I want you out of my town now!"

Ben just looked at him. He thought about saying something. He thought about publicly reminding him of their agreement. He thought of trying to humiliate him in some way before he left town. He even thought about refusing to leave just to make a point. But in the split second that it took for all those thoughts to roll around in his brain, Gonzales gave a slight jerk to his head. Ben did not miss it. He looked in the direction Gonzales indicated and saw Juanita in the back of the boss's car. She looked like she had been crying.

Had this devil changed his mind? Was he trying to send Ben away without his sister? Was he trying to send a warning to Ben to cooperate? To let Gonzales have the upper hand and preserve his self-proclaimed authority?

Ben did not have time to decide. The next words out of Gonzales's mouth sealed the deal. "Not only are you to leave immediately, you will take that no-good excuse of a daughter of mine with you. You two deserve each other. No man around here will have her, and I am tired of supporting her. Good luck with her. Just remember, when I send something away, it is gone for good. If either of you ever try to return, you will wish you had not!"

With that, Gonzales opened his car door, grabbed Juanita by the hair, and pulled her out of the car and onto the ground. He walked around to the driver's side, got in, and sped away.

"You heard him," said the foreman, "get going!"

Ben had wanted to run after Gonzales and put his fist into his loud mouth. But instead, he went to his sister and gently lifted her up. He could see the red mark across her face where she had been slapped violently. Her tears flowed unbidden. Ben gently rubbed them away.

"Go on! Get!" yelled the foreman.

"Gladly," Ben said under his breath. Taking Juanita by the elbow, he led her to his car. "We are on our way to freedom," he told her on the way. "The time for crying is over. Your new life awaits."

CHAPTER

## 32

One month later, Ben sat with Juanita in Uncle Lewis's living room. The time between now and when they drove away from the Mexican factory was a bit of a blur. Ben now understood why Uncle Lewis could never fully explain how it had happened that Ben's mother and grandmother had been granted asylum and been free to pursue new lives in the United States. Miraculously, the same thing had happened for Juanita.

Ben would be forever grateful to Phoebe Collins for her influence in making it happen. By the time Ben and Juanita had gotten to the border, God had paved their way. The agent who was on duty in their crossing lane was a familiar face. He had crossed Ben back and forth many times. "I've been waiting for you," he had said with a grin on his face. "My wife works with Phoebe."

A sigh of relief escaped Ben's lips and all he could say was, "Praise God!"

Juanita had been completely oblivious to everything going on. There were so many new sights, so many new things she could never have imagined. She had never even seen a real paved road before. Ben had been trying to prepare her for her new world as they drove the short way to the border that would take them into Texas, but how could he have ever explained all this. Even with his detailed explanations, this was beyond all that her imagination had been able to formulate.

"Come on, sis," Ben coaxed as they were instructed to park and go with the border agent. "Remember what we talked about and what you will need to tell them."

Inside the facility, Ben and Juanita had been shown to a small interview room. A translator was there, and a tape recorder was set up to have a permanent record transcribed for her case. The way had been paved for her request for asylum, and the drawn-out interview process that was usually necessary to determine an alien's status and subsequent detention or deportation had been nearly nonexistent. Phoebe had really come through. The papers were all filled out and needed only her testimony and signature. Ben had already filled out the paperwork to be her sponsor. Whatever needed to take place behind the scenes had been rushed in part due to Maria's and Consuelo's cases. Reviewing what they had experienced at the hands of Pedro Gonzalez helped to paint a picture of what Juanita had probably experienced. Her testimony and Ben's clinched the deal.

And now, a month later, the miraculous was still unbelievable. Not only had the Savior freed Juanita from her physical prison, He also freed her from her spiritual one. Just a week ago, she asked Jesus to save her, to be her Lord. She was eagerly celebrating two new lives. Ben marveled at the change in her. He could never have imagined that the meek, sad, hopeless woman he met in that cantina just over a year ago could have been transformed into the vibrant, lively, beautiful woman he saw before him. The same abused broken woman who got in his car to leave the only life she had ever known had become the woman she was meant to be. If only his mom—their mom—could see her now.

The thought of Maria brought a bit of sadness to Ben's heart, even with the celebratory atmosphere in the room. Uncle Lewis noticed and gave him a reassuring nod as if to say, *I understand. I wish they were all here too.*

CHAPTER

33

Juanita had indeed become a new creature, not only spiritually, but in every aspect of her life. The saints at church adored her. Because of the diversity of ethnicity in that area of Texas, it was not uncommon for churches to have bilingual services. Faith Community was too small of a church to warrant separate worship services, but there was a small group class that was held in Spanish. Juanita attended faithfully and soon had more friends with whom she could easily communicate than she had in all of Mexico.

Ben was pleased when Juanita wanted to take classes to learn English. It seemed she had no regrets whatsoever about the new life that had been thrust upon her.

*Everything works together for good,* Ben thought as he watched his sister. As he had planned, Ben threw himself into his sister's life, but it quickly became apparent that Juanita did not need so much focused attention from him. She had truly blossomed. It was time to let go a bit and let her fly solo. Sadness took over Ben's emotions as he pondered letting her go. No, he would not be out of her life completely, but hovering around her like some kind of parental helicopter was out of the question. Maybe he should just go back home for a while.

Ben had taken Juanita to his childhood home once she had settled into her new life. He showed her pictures of her mom. He let her touch all his mom's things in hopes that she would identify with this woman who had loved her. Juanita tried her best to listen to Ben's stories as if she had really been a part of this family. She longed to please her brother and somehow assuage some of the guilt he needlessly had taken from his mother concerning her. But her mind drifted back to her new friends and the life she had begun in Texas.

Ben could tell that Juanita's heart and mind were elsewhere. This had been *his* life, and try as he might, he could not make it hers. He suggested that Juanita choose some things of Maria's to remind her that her mother had never forgotten her and that her dying wish had been to reunite her with family. Maria had known that Ben would love his sister.

Ben had called Uncle Lewis a few days before. He noticed how lonely his uncle had sounded now that everyone had gone. Ben told his uncle how sad Juanita was and how hard she tried to hide it from him. Over the course of the conversation, Uncle Lewis offered to have Juanita come and stay with him until she could decide what she wanted to do with her life. Relief flooded Ben's soul, although he had not realized how stressed he had been. *All things,* Ben thought with a smile. How long had it been since a smile had come so easily? He immediately knew in his heart that this was the answer to his prayers.

After Juanita had chosen a few of her mother's things, Ben approached her with the idea of her going back to Texas. He noticed a smile cross her face before she could make it stop or replace it with a more solemn appearance. She did not want to hurt her brother or seem ungrateful for she truly was grateful for her rescue. Even though she had not known she needed to be rescued. This new life was full of wonder, friendship, and beautiful things. Jesus was filling her with a peace she had not known existed and yet could feel so palpably. She did not want to disappoint Ben, but oh, how much she wanted to go.

"What do you think, brother," she began, "do you want me to go back to Texas?"

"Well, Uncle Lewis did sound awfully lonely there by himself. I'm sure he would appreciate some company."

"I think I would like that as well." Juanita hung her head just a little when she confessed that she wanted to return. Ben noticed and tried to make it into a positive thing.

"You know, I really have to get back to work and to my normal routine. I have taken way too much time off. How about if we take one more trip back to see Uncle Lewis? You can stay with him while I come back here and do what I need to do. I will be only a phone call away. You can think about what you would like to do and where you would like to live. You can live here or just visit whenever you want, but we will always be family. I love you, sis." He gave her a hug. He could feel tears from her face wetting his shoulder.

"Happy tears, I hope?" he asked as he pulled back a little.

"Happy tears," she said with a smile.

And so, here they were. Back in Texas. Juanita seemed so happy. Uncle Lewis seemed happy to have her around. The friends who came over to welcome her back seemed happy to catch her up on everything she had missed. Juanita couldn't keep from smiling.

That left Ben alone with his thoughts. *Yes, I have to go home, back to my life. How will I bear it without Jenny?*

Ben could hear a still, small voice in his spirit instructing him, to *Listen to your heart. What is broken, God can make whole. What is shattered, God can put back together.* Then the Lord reminded Ben that his life was not in his circumstances. His life was in God.

Startled at what he thought he had just heard Ben looked once more around the room. It was true. There was life all around him. There was fulfillment all around him. Circumstances had been changed, and it was good; it was very good.

Ben began saying his goodbyes, resolved to keep in touch, and made his way to his car. A new chapter was about to begin.

# EPILOGUE

It was the anniversary of the last time he saw Jenny. It was a day filled with sadness and regret. Ben could hardly bear to think of her, so great was his love for the one he had lost. And yet, he couldn't stay away. He went to the square and sat on the same bench where they spent their final moments together and gazed at the same gazebo. He couldn't really focus on the gazebo, or on anything else surrounding him for that matter, because of the tears that came so freely. Ben didn't even attempt to brush them away. He let them fall unashamedly down his cheeks and onto the green and blue scarf he ever-so-gently held in his gloved hands.

It was her scarf. His beloved Jenny had left it on the bench the night she walked away from him forever. He could not bear to call her back on that night to return it and then to have to say goodbye all over again. Now he could not bear to part with it at all. He hadn't thought of it since that night. It had been too warm in Mexico for his heavy coat, and tonight was the first time he had worn it. He found it in his pocket as he made his way to the square. Was this God's way of speaking to him ever so gently? Or was it God's way of reminding him of how life could have been if Ben had only accepted Christ's forgiveness earlier?

Ben refused to believe God was punishing him, so he chose to believe God was simply reminding him of His goodness that was such a part of Jenny's life. Still, Ben questioned. Why couldn't he have realized what he was missing back then? In spite of his resolve to not question God's timing in drawing Ben to Himself, he couldn't help thinking what-if? *What if I had found my relationship with Christ back when Jenny first explained my need for Him? What if I could have told Jenny that I shared her faith?* Jenny had told him that she could never marry someone who did not share her faith in God—someone who had never accepted Christ, someone like him.

The tears came even harder until Ben felt there couldn't possibly be any tears left in him. He was weary. He wanted to leave this place but couldn't convince his body to cooperate. The sky darkened. Snow began to fall. Beautiful crisp snowflakes sparkled like diamonds in the lights surrounding the square. Jenny had called it Christmas snow. It was the same kind of snow that fell that night. It seemed like a lifetime ago, yet at the same time, it felt like yesterday. Juanita had been his welcome distraction once he found out about Jenny, but Juanita was now safe, and his life had returned to normal. His life had returned to the past. His life had returned to the moment he said goodbye to Jenny.

It was that time of the year, when the days were short and darkness came early. Jenny had stayed late at the library and was now cutting across the square on her way back to her apartment. The lights bordering the square had just come on, and Jenny could see the first flakes of snow bedazzled by the lights and sparkling like diamonds. *Ah, Christmas snow*, she thought with a smile.

As Jenny approached the gazebo, her steps slowed. A strange sensation overtook her, but she could not identify it. It was akin to fear, but she was not afraid. She walked this way all the time. It was a safe college town, and she could come up with no reason to be afraid. So what was this feeling? She edged closer to the gazebo. Ahead of her she could see a man sitting on a bench. Still not able to identify anything that should cause her to be fearful, she found herself stopped in her own tracks and within an arm's reach of the gazebo. She was out of his field of vision, yet she could see him plainly. *Lord, protect me*, she instinctively prayed.

*I am with you always.* The biblical verse Matthew 28:20 came into her spirit. Jenny began to feel more at ease, yet she still did not leave her vantage point. She studied the lone figure on the bench. He was looking down at his hands. *What is he holding?* She wondered. *Is that a scarf? I used to have one like that. Is that my scarf?*

A brief moment of whatever the emotion was that was akin to fear but not quite fear engulfed her again. She wondered if the man could be a stalker.

"Lord?" Jenny breathed.

A quiet response came to her spirit, reminding her that He was there and to look closer. Jenny looked again at the man on the bench holding the scarf. His head was down. His shoulders shook just the tiniest bit. *Is he weeping?* Jenny wondered. Compassion replaced her uneasiness. She looked again. She noticed his gloved hands as he raised one to wipe his tears.

*I know those gloves. Where do I know them? Where have I seen them? Why are they familiar?* A recurring dream came back to her. A dream where she was sitting on a bench with a man who meant the world to her. His arm was around her shoulder, and her gloved hand held his gloved hand, the gloves she had given him for Christmas. It was always a dream where she could not see his face, could not remember him at all, could not remember the before or after of that one moment captured in her memory. Ben.

Suddenly, like a great avalanche, memories flooded her whole being. So great was the force and magnitude of so many memories that Jenny's knees buckled, and she reached out for the gazebo. Hundreds of broken memory fibers reconnected in an instant! She knew, beyond a shadow of a doubt, that God had answered her constant prayer. Everything she had blocked about this man came back in a flood so overwhelming she thought her mind incapable of surviving the immensity of it. She leaned with her back against the gazebo. She was exhausted with the effort. *What now?* She wondered.

Ben rose to leave. He couldn't bear to leave, but he couldn't bear to stay. If only he could see her one more time. He gazed over the square. His glance lingered on the gazebo. A shadow moved. A figure emerged. A woman began to walk toward him. His thoughts screamed *Jenny!* But it could not be. God could not be so cruel as to send a mirage to torture him further. He blinked several times, but still she walked toward him. Seconds seemed like hours. He couldn't move, couldn't look away. Still she walked toward him.

Jenny remembered it all. Every single detail. She bowed her head and whispered, "Thank You, Lord."

Strength returned to her legs. Peace flooded her soul. She took a tentative step … and then another … and then a more confident step …

and another. The space between them began to close. She saw him raise his eyes to meet hers. He did not move, but Jenny did. Closer and closer they came until they stood face-to-face.

Years of frustration evaporated for Jenny. She smiled.

Years of anguish screamed within Ben, yet he could not speak. He struggled with this vision, this mirage that was impossible yet so very real. Jenny reached out her hand. Ben took it in his and looked down at this clasp of impossibility. Slowly he looked up into her eyes. Reality began to set in.

Ben reached for her other hand. They stood hand in hand and face-to-face, yet neither could speak for fear of breaking the spell. For fear that the other would disappear. Magical Christmas snow fell all around them.

"I found the Lord," Ben whispered.

In that instant, all their hopes and dreams and wishes and prayers had come to pass, and they melted into each other's arms.

# DISCUSSION QUESTIONS

1.  How did Jenny feel when she first discovered that she had lost her memory? How would you have felt?

2.  Could you feel Jenny's trepidation when she left the hospital and hoped she would recognize her own home?

3.  How did Jenny feel about not being able to recall anything about Ben and not being able to find out anything about him? How would you have reacted?

4.  What do you think kept Jenny's frustrations in check? How do you keep your frustrations in check?

5.  When did Jenny come to the conclusion that she could do nothing on her own to find answers? How did she cope with that decision?

6.  How do you think Jenny might have felt after her discussion with her mother about the couple wanting to join the church and realizing there may still be other things she did not remember besides Ben?

7.  Grace did not consider herself a hypocrite or prejudicial and could not see how Jenny could possibly see her that way. Is there anything in your

own life that may be considered prejudice or hypocrisy by others? How might we be blinded to it? Can you give an example?

8. In what ways could you identify with Jenny?

9. In what ways could you identify with Ben?

10. How easy was it for Ben to watch his mother suffer? Have you been in a similar situation? How did you cope?

11. How do you feel about Maria asking Ben to promise to search for and rescue his sister?

12. Knowing his mother's story, how do you think Ben wanted to act toward Gonzales, and how did he act? What would you have done? Did Ben have a choice?

13. How did Ben cope with losing Jenny before finding the Lord and then after finding the Lord?

14. Ben had his regrets. How did he cope? How do you cope with regrets? What can be done to alleviate them?

15. How did you like the ending of the book? Would you have ended the story differently? Why or why not?

CPSIA information can be obtained
at www.ICGtesting.com
Printed in the USA
BVHW051011250922
647944BV00005B/97